HUTCHISON STREET

The following is a work of fiction. Many of the locations are real, although
not necessarily as portrayed, but all characters and events are fictional
and any resemblance to actual events or people, living or dead, is purely
coincidental.

Prepared for the press by Carmelita McGrath.
Cover photo by Lindsay Crysler
Cover design by Debbie Geltner
Book design by WildElement.ca

Library and Archives Canada Cataloguing in Publication

Farhoud, Abla, 1945-
[Sourire de la petite juive. English]
        Hutchison Street / Abla Farhoud ; translated by Judith
Weisz Woodsworth.
Translation of: Le sourire de la petite juive.
Issued in print and electronic formats.
ISBN 978-1-988130-74-3 (softcover).--ISBN 978-1-988130-75-0
(HTML).--ISBN 978-1-988130-76-7 (Kindle).--ISBN 978-1-988130-77-4
(PDF)
        I. Woodsworth, Judith, translator II. Title. III. Title: Sourire
de la petite juive. English
PS8561.A687S6813 2018   C843'.54   C2017-906569-6
                                                 C2017-906570-X

Printed and bound in Canada.

The publisher gratefully acknowledges the support of the Government of
Canada through the Canada Council for the Arts, the Canada Book Fund,
and Livres Canada Books, and of the Government of Quebec through the
Société de développement des entreprises culturelles (SODEC).
We acknowledge the financial support of the Government of Canada
through the National Translation Program for Book Publishing, an initiative
of the Roadmap for Canada's Official Languages 2013-2018: Education, Immigration, Communities, for our translation activities.

Linda Leith Publishing
Montreal
www.lindaleith.com

MAY 24 2018

HUTCHISON STREET

A novel

ABLA FARHOUD

TRANSLATION BY JUDITH WEISZ WOODSWORTH

This is a work of fiction. I apologize in advance if any residents of Hutchison Street were to recognize themselves and feel offended. I would be delighted, on the other hand, if some people did recognize themselves and felt flattered by the way in which they have been portrayed. The names of all the characters have of course been changed. I am pleased to acknowledge my debt to the women and men of Hutchison Street.

A.F.

Stories turn their back on *the* truth. The truth of a story lies in its capacity to create meaning. It thus stands as our supreme connection with the world because it is the freest, the least censored among them.

Thierry Hentsch
Truth or Death

Isaiah asked him, "What hast thou to do with the secrets of the All-merciful?"

Berakhot 10a (Talmud)

PROLOGUE

Last night, I dreamed that I had as many children as books. Or rather, that my books were my flesh-and-blood children. I looked at them, all lined up together on one row of my bookshelf. They were on their best behaviour, standing in order from the eldest to the littlest one. My bed was set up in my office, I don't know why. An immense bed in an immense room as big as my entire apartment. The room was empty except for shelves crammed with books, which lined three of the walls. The fourth wall was punctuated by four giant windows extending from the floor to the ceiling.

A magnificent light poured into the room from the street, even though I knew it was night time. I was lying in my enormous bed and I was calling out, "Children, I am thirsty, I would like a glass of water. I'm thirsty, kids, I want some water." No one came. "Paper prog-e-ny," I uttered with indescribable emotion. Fate, sorrow, choices, destiny, winning and losing, with death lurking at the end of the road. All of these thoughts were tangled up in my mind.

I woke up, very thirsty, reciting those two words aloud

so I would not forget them. I took out my notebook and quickly jotted down the words "paper progeny," wondering whether I was sorry that I had not had children, that I had put everything into my writing. Everything. Body and soul, my entire life. Everything. My friends, my lovers, the children I could have had – all of them had come SECOND to my irrepressible desire to write, write, write and then write some more. In my heart, in my mind, there was only room for my paper progeny.

Can a single thing – such as a profession, a career, a love affair, a passion, a place, or a God – be worth devoting an entire life to?

I think about myself and the Hasidic community. The Hebrew word, transcribed as *Hasid* (Hassid, Chasid, Chassid) in the singular and *Hasidim* in the plural, signifies "pious." Hasidim spend their whole life dedicated to God. Every feature of their life is guided by the presence of God. Everything is bound up with this God without a name, referred to simply as *Hashem* or "the name."

Since the age of twenty-five, my own Hashem has been writing. I've just substituted writing for the concept of Hashem.

They say that the Jews, and Hasidim in particular, have a portable homeland, the Torah. Mine is just as portable; it regulates my life, my every action, and all of my thoughts.

A common expression comes to mind: don't put all your eyes in one basket ... In writing this down, I have made a slip of the tongue. I've written *eyes* instead of *eggs*.

4

It's true, my eyes have always been focused on the same basket. It's a bottomless, boundless basket into which I dig deep, in search of an image or a word to use in building a sentence, a paragraph, a page, a chapter and a book.

My thirst for saying, telling, seeking, understanding and finding has never been fully quenched. I feel like I'm always missing the point. And so I begin another book, hoping to find the answer, but without knowing whether I'll recognize it when I see it, and, if I do, how I will put it into words.

Perhaps all is not lost. In my dream, there were four large windows and lots of light. The windows faced Hutchison Street. The sounds of the street and the light shining in from outside are coming back to me now. Such a beautiful light.

THE MILE END SIDE

THE DIARY OF HINDA ROCHEL

Dear Diary,

It has been a long time since I last wrote because I am never home alone. My younger brothers are playing in the backyard, the baby is asleep, and my older brother and my father have not come home yet. I think I will cry if I don't talk to anyone. Luckily I have my diary. My mother has gone out to buy a big pot to cook meat in. It was my fault that she had to throw out everything in the pot and the pot itself because I had contaminated it by using butter instead of margarine. It was a stupid mistake, my God, how awful. But it was just because I wasn't paying attention, may God forgive me. When I realized what I had done, I acted as if nothing had happened. I continued to stir the beef stew just as Mama had asked me to. I opened all the windows and the kitchen door and prayed that no one would notice anything. Because we don't have a lot of money. What a waste to throw away a nice pot like that, with a thick bottom, along with all the good meat that was in it, and good vegetables, and the stainless steel spoon I was using to stir it with. But in spite of my prayers, the smell of butter mixed with meat reached Mama's nostrils. She was in my brothers' bedroom at the front of the house looking after the baby who was crying. She could smell the forbidden mixture. Other people would have liked that smell. Me too, if I had been brought up by the Goys. But that's the problem. We are not used to it. Sometimes, especially in the summer when the windows are open, I catch the smell of this very mixture coming from the houses of the neighbours. And I don't like it. But I was still praying that no one would notice. My mother came running with my baby brother in her arms and she yelled at me, "Oy vey! Oy vey! What are you doing, you bad girl? May Hashem forgive you, you have contaminated my pot, my best pot, and the only one big enough to feed all of you." Oy vey! Oy vey! I don't like those words. I would have liked to tell her that God would understand and that He would overlook the sacrilege just this once because He knows that I'm still a child and I didn't do it on purpose. Sometimes children are pardoned for things that grown-ups are not. But with my mother, you don't fool around with the rules. You are not allowed to mix milk and meat, period! Never. If she had to choose between eating contaminated food or dying, I'm sure my mother would choose to die. I was surprised, because my mother is not often mad at me. "Oy vey! Oy vey!" she said, as she usually does when she is angry, but she didn't punish me. She just said, "Look after your little brother. I'm going out to buy a pot. When he's asleep peel the vegetables that are left." Moishy fell asleep quickly, so I was happy. I began to write, right away. And when I start to write, I forget about everything.

FRANÇOISE CAMIRAND

She came from an average family, neither rich nor poor. There was nothing dramatic or remarkable about her family, which was like hundreds of others in Duvernay, where she was born. Everything was predictable, conventional and stable. Everything conspired, in fact, to make the life of an intelligent, curious and lively little girl turn out just a tad monotonous. You could even say boring. Her father had been working at the Saint-Vincent-de-Paul Penitentiary for ages. Her mother stayed home, looked after the children and kept the house clean and tidy. It was a house without knickknacks, where colouring was off limits because it made things dirty. It was so spic-and-span that you could eat off the floor, as people used to say in those days, except that you were only allowed to eat sitting up straight, at the table, with a napkin tied around your neck or placed neatly in your lap. No one ever told stories, and jokes were few and far between, although the occasional nervous twitter could be heard. It was so dull you could die. The two boys slept in one bedroom, the two girls in another, with their parents in the master bedroom. Out front there was an unbelievably green lawn. There was a small backyard, which was just as uncluttered as the house was inside, with no toys lying around and no swings. Françoise was the third child, followed by a sister who was less than a year younger, who was always getting in her hair.

The year she was born, there was a big change in the Camirand household. A television set arrived – a large, gleaming piece of furniture that took pride of place right in the middle of the living room – and it transformed the life of every member of the family. This became their only form of "entertainment" because, apart from the one-week vacation they took every year in Old Orchard, they had none.

Françoise adored the television. Seated in her highchair, even before she learned to talk, she already recognized the characters in the programs. She stared at the TV blankly, occasionally burbling in appreciation, watching everything the family watched. Along with her brothers and her sister, she was mesmerized by everyone in the kids' program called the surprise box, *La boîte à surprise*. But her favourite character was the living doll Fanfreluche, who was so talented she could pop out of a big book, slip back in again, and then set off in search of adventure. As Françoise grew older, she became more and more entranced by television because she was beginning to understand the stories and could even predict how they would unfold. It was fun to try to guess how the TV series would turn out, and when she was dead on, she was very proud of herself.

It was television that triggered her interest in captivating stories, in which her beloved characters sprang to life, but her taste for writing came from reading. It happened at school. At home, there were very few books. Her parents had never read to her and had not even told her bedtime stories. She was the one who told stories to her sister to get her to stop babbling. Her father would read biographies of famous men, but her mother claimed that she didn't have time for "that sort of thing." The only time of day when Madame Camirand allowed her backside to sink into the sofa was when she was watching television. She was never idle, though. To keep from biting her nails or from smoking – the only two little bad habits you could fault the queen bee with – she kept her hands occupied by crocheting or knitting.

School was a real liberation for Françoise. She learned to read at an astonishing pace, so fast and so well that her teacher, who was clever and wholeheartedly dedicated to her pupils, slipped her books while the other girls mumbled their way through easy reading exercises. She would have gone to school on Saturday and Sunday if she could. She was still in grade one when she discovered the pleasure of reading – in her case it would be more accurate to say her love of books. In the difficult years that followed, it was always reading that kept her afloat. The pleasure of writing came a little later, in grade six to be precise, when the children had to write about what they had done on their summer holidays. With unimagined joy, Françoise began to invent the vacation of her dreams, extraordinary holidays, but plausible ones, which all the girls, and not just her, would have loved to have had. This made her friends believe that everything she wrote was true, that it had actually happened that way. She didn't dare to contradict them. That day, she experienced something new: she discovered how much she enjoyed making other people believe in something, how much she liked telling a story and sharing good times that she had dreamed up all by herself, in her own head. The pleasure she derived from writing endured, but it also turned into a need and a desire that was renewed with each new book, although after completing each of her novels she would also be overcome by periods of extreme fatigue.

Françoise Camirand was sixteen years old when she left home, escaping from her parents and the suburb she so despised. Before leaving, she wrote a letter addressed to Monsieur and Madame Léopold Camirand, leaving out her mother's first name out of deference to her personal choice. On the rare occasion when she had seen her mother write her name on a letter, or one of her report cards, she would sign it as Madame Léopold Camirand, as if she had forgotten her given name. In fact, even her husband called her *maman*. In her letter, Françoise told them not to worry. She said everything would be okay, and, in particular, asked them not to go looking for her because she NEVER wanted to live in Duvernay anymore. To be polite, she did not add "or with you." When she arrived in Montreal, she slipped the letter into a shiny red Canada Post mailbox and ran off to join the gang of friends at the Hutchison Street apartment they had all rented together.

She has been living here, alone, ever since she published her first successful book. Her roommates have been replaced by cats and magnificent plants, a desk and bookshelves. Every Wednesday afternoon, she invites the grade-two class from Lambert-Closse School to come over. After the kind of childhood she had, it has felt like sweet revenge to be surrounded by the children she likes to call her "best friends," who come to have a snack and draw while she reads to them from the world's most beautiful children's books. She reads stories from all over, stories like *The Little Prince* by Saint-Exupéry, which they ask for over and over again. With the children seated around her on the floor – eating, colouring and laughing – she is happy. They take delight in everything and are thrilled when she reads them something scary. After they leave, and before she cleans up, she thinks about her mother, who would have a fit if she saw what shape her place was in.

Her first year in Montreal was exciting, a time of overindulgence, friends, alcohol, and parties stretching into the wee hours of the morning. She drank life in like a prisoner who had just broken out of jail. She went from party to party. All that mattered was having a good time and making enough money to keep on having a good time. But, gradually, she grew tired of partying, which left a bitter taste in her mouth. Her waitressing job, which she had liked at first, was becoming routine and pointless, except for the money she earned. She began to feel empty, and angry too. Surely she hadn't given up everything she

hated about her life just to end up like this? Had she merely jumped from the frying pan into the fire? When she
was little, she had had dreams. One, at least, that she had
cherished since she was in sixth grade.

The more she tried to suppress her anxiety, the more it
grew. She tried to steady her nerves with alcohol, but that
only made her drink more and more. Deep down, she
knew what she had to do, she knew she was talented. She
still had a burning desire to write, but she wasn't ready to
take the plunge. A hundred miles from school, where any
old composition would have made a good impression, she
was now in the playground of grown-ups, who could eat
you alive, tear your work apart and destroy you without
giving it a second thought. Her insides churned with fear
just thinking about it.

For years, she had rushed headlong into self-destruction, leading an ever more dissipated life. And then, all
at once, she felt as though a thick veil had lifted. For the
first time, she was able stare fear in the face. "I don't want
to die, I don't want to die," she could hear herself say. "I
don't want to die before I start writing." That day, it so
happened that her roommates were not at home. She was
alone in the eight-room apartment. She walked up and
down, and around in circles, pacing back and forth and
repeating, "I don't want to die." All of a sudden, without
thinking, she rushed into her bedroom and picked up a
pad of paper she had bought some time before. And without waiting a second longer, she sat down at the kitchen
table and began to write like a madwoman.

Her first novel had been buried deep inside her since the age of fifteen, and she wrote it in seven months. Her fears came and went. She didn't have time to be afraid anymore. She didn't have time to feel sorry for herself or to try to conquer her fears by drinking. Françoise was operating in crisis mode. It was either write or die. Little by little, the pleasure of writing crept back. The joy of imagining and inventing worlds, of bringing herself into the world, triumphed and replaced her fear of dying.

Her suffering could have destroyed her, but she used it as the raw material for her writing. She would mine the suffering, extracting what she needed, turning it into words and transferring it to one of her characters. As long as she came back up to the surface as quickly as possible. In the beginning, she was scared to death that the dark thoughts would pull her under like quicksand.

Her fifteenth novel has just come out. It is an ambitious and whimsical story of a family, beginning in Gaspésie in 1940 and ending in Montreal in 2001. A voluminous book that took a long time to write, it was a lot of fun but it has drained all her energy. She feels tired, not out of steam yet, but almost. The promotional events are over, too, and the novel is on its own. There are no new projects in the works, nothing in her head or on her worktable. Instead, she's had a lot of dreams. Dreams have always been important to her, that's often how novels are born. Yet, at this particular moment, she feels in limbo, as if she were floating in space, weightless, with nothing to hang on to.

For several nights, she has been dreaming about the people on her street, especially the Hasidic people. They're dreams, not nightmares, not yet. Why the Hasidim? She has been living in the neighbourhood for thirty-nine years, and she has seen them every day without ever dreaming about them. Yet now, increasingly, they are beginning to haunt her. She dreams that they are parading down Hutchison Street playing raucous music. The neighbours are going out into the street to dance with them. A fight breaks out, with the rabbi just barely managing to rescue the scrolls of the Torah. A bus is filled with women travelling to New York to find husbands, but they turn back because they want to marry Québécois and learn to speak French. Two young men with sidelocks are kissing each other right out in the street, creating a scandal in the community. Last night, she dreamed that the little Hasidic girl came over and rang her doorbell. In her dream, the girl was the spitting image of Françoise. She smiled at Françoise and headed straight for her computer as if she knew her way around the house. With knitted brows, she typed page after page without even looking up. What would Françoise dream of next?

Strange. She feels strange. Something barely perceptible is shifting inside her … she feels like she is drifting in a new direction … She says, aloud, as if she needs to hear herself say it over and over again, "I will never again write the same way." She is not repudiating what she has written before. She would defend every word, but she wants nothing more to do with that mode of writing, with writing obsessively. After all, she has nothing more to prove to anybody – except a little bit to herself, still. Fifteen novels, several short story collections and some children's books. Her novels have been translated into several languages, and some have been made into films. If she could only find the time to live differently, to write differently. She is fifty-five years old, a perfect age to change.

She's like the inveterate drunk who gets up the morning after a terrible binge and says, "I will never drink again." After she finished a novel, she would say, "I don't want to work myself to death anymore. I don't want to write each book as if it were my last." But it has just been wishful thinking, a resolution that quickly evaporates. All it would take was for one new project to capture her heart and mind, and she was hooked, carried away by what she was going to discover along the way.

She goes out onto her balcony with a glass of wine in her hand. It's nice out. The little Jewish girl she dreamed about last night is sitting on the stoop across the street, reading a book. In her dream, the girl seemed older than she actually is, she looked almost like an adolescent. Her younger brother is playing next to her. An even younger child is peering out the window. He is rapping on the windowpane because he wants to come outside too.

Françoise takes a sip of wine and looks down over the street. The girl is dragging her brother into the house because her mother has just called them in.

She can't remember having spoken to one single member of the Hasidic community, or even having smiled at anyone. Never, not once in thirty-nine years. Actually, she has never even made the effort, as if she has always known that it would do no good. That's why she's puzzled by her dreams. Why now?

The first time she saw a foreigner, she was about ten years old. One afternoon, a new girl came into the classroom. She was called Francesca, the Italian name for Françoise, something she learned much later when she and Francesca became friends. She remembers going home that day and writing about it in her diary, which she kept hidden under her mattress: "My God, how unhappy Francesca must be. All she knows how to say is hello. That's all. What will she do when she has to go pee? Tomorrow I'm going to teach her how to say, Miss, may I go to the washroom, please?" Françoise smiles as she thinks about what she was like as a little girl, about Francesca who couldn't answer the teacher's questions, about the year they spent together on Hutchison Street in an apartment filled with people, about the angst which consumed her for so long, and which still creeps up on her from time to time.

Hutchison is quiet. A few cars cruise by almost soundlessly, while young Hasidim, their heads bowed and their foreheads glistening with sweat, scurry along the street in their everyday clothes. The first time she laid eyes on them, she was bowled over. Every time she ran into them during the first year, it was as if she were seeing them for the first time. She couldn't get used to it. Gradually, they became part of the landscape, but not the culture.

It was not the fact that they were foreign that baffled her. There were plenty of foreigners around and she loved the neighbourhood for that very reason. Foreigners take on the characteristics of their adoptive country and give something back to the country in return. With time, they become different from the way they once were, that's just how it is. Hasidic Jews have been living here for generations, and they are still the same as ever. They are a homogeneous group, and that's what she finds surprising, not their strangeness. She can't conceive of them as individuals. Instead, she sees them as a monolithic group, which has remained cut off from the outside world, and untouched by it. But why is she just starting to dream about them now, after thirty-nine years of living alongside them?

Her neighbours are outside on their balconies, enjoying the fine weather. Some of them are already wearing shorts, as if they hadn't a second to lose. The beautiful young woman next door has invited friends over. They are going in and out of her place, a beer in one hand, talking loudly and laughing, already tipsy. They are probably celebrating spring. Any excuse for a party, as she well knows, because not too long ago she was their age.

She takes another sip of wine and thinks about all the people she has rubbed shoulders with for so many years, without even knowing their names. She thinks about one person she has known since she was a baby. Francoise used to see her when she was a child riding her tricycle, then as a little girl going back and forth to school, then as a young woman kissing a boy, and later on with her arms wrapped around someone else.

At the corner of Bernard, people are going in and out of the TD Bank, while others are rifling through bins in front of the grocery store.

The Hasidic girl steps out of her house, the fingers of her right hand lightly brushing the *mezuzah* as she closes the front door. For a split second her gaze meets Françoise's. The girl runs toward Bernard clutching some money in her hand. She crosses the street and enters the corner store.

Françoise mulls over her dream and, once again, it strikes her that she and the little girl look very much alike. At least in her dreams.

THE DIARY OF HINDA ROCHEL

Today, I got a big shock. It was awful.

I've been looking forward to getting a minute to myself so I can write down what I saw on my way home from school.

Usually, I walk home with my friend Naomi, but she wasn't at school today, I'm not sure why. I don't often get a chance to walk alone. When I'm not with Naomi, I'm always with my brothers or, even worse, with my parents and the whole family. I love to walk alone, to have the time to look at people. Not just the people in my community, I know those ones by heart, but the others. I was walking slowly. It was nice out, and I saw young girls and boys who were my age. They were out walking, running, chasing each other and holding hands. No, to be honest, they were a little older than me. At least thirteen years old. Even fourteen.

I followed them, but I kept my distance. They were walking quickly. Except for a boy and a girl who were taking their time. They were holding hands, and then they put their arms around one another.

I saw the boy stop right in the middle of the sidewalk. He pulled the girl up against his chest, held her tight, and kissed her on the lips. A shiver ran down my spine. I felt paralysed.

The girl tipped her head back and was kissing the boy as if it was the last thing she wanted to do before she died. I was sure she was going to run out of breath any minute. It was beautiful. No, it was disgusting. I was standing there, not far from them, and I didn't know which way to turn. I wanted to disappear, to close my eyes, but I kept on staring at them. May God forgive me, I pretended that I was her. I was ashamed to look. It was beautiful and ugly at the same time. I would have died if the boy had kissed me, I know I would. For sure, I'd be dead.

Then the blood began flowing through my veins again. The wheels in my head started to turn again and I came back to my senses. I quickly stepped down from the sidewalk and onto the road, to avoid the boy and girl. I walked around them, turned down Hutchison and ran home. Luckily, our house is just a few steps away from Bernard, where I had seen them kissing, on the corner, right there on the corner.

It's a good thing that I know how to write in French. That way, my family can't read my diary. Sometimes I pretend to be doing homework, but I'm actually writing in my diary. I can't help feeling a bit nervous, though. The other day, my big brother got suspicious. What's wrong? he asked. He thought I looked funny, different than I usually look when I'm doing my homework. I told him that I had a composition to write in French. He said, poor you, good luck with that. He hates French. There aren't many people in our community who like the French language. I'm different, but it wasn't on purpose. It's because of Gabrielle Roy. I really like her a lot. I have read Bonheur d'occasion at least a dozen times.[1]

24

WILLA COLERIDGE

If you counted up all the lost smiles, if you could deposit them into a bank account, Willa Coleridge would certainly be a millionaire. Just counting the times she smiled at the growing number of Hasidim on Hutchison Street would have been enough to make her a rich person or else a saint. All the other people who lived on the street had given up. They had soon come to the conclusion that it was a lost cause, that their smiles were wasted, everyone except Willa, who was unwilling to admit defeat. But she could not understand why those people, who were her neighbours and whom she had never hurt in any way, did not smile back at her.

And as long as she didn't understand why not, she was going to keep on doing what she had always done.

You might think that she was born that way, always smiling, but that wouldn't be completely accurate. She was born black, that much is true, but she smiled by choice, as a way of life, as a way of combatting the dreariness and hardships of life, and as of a way of reaching out to others. A smile leaves the door open to a possible relationship. Even when she was little, she knew how to use her smile to cheer herself up, and it had made her life easier. At school, she chose to smile rather than cry when faced with her huge learning disabilities, telling herself that she would get through by working harder. And she succeeded. She was never first in her class, but she passed. With time, this became her way of being, her way of connecting to the world and her way of expressing herself. I smile, therefore I am, with no intention of paraphrasing Descartes whom she had never heard of. The Bible was the only book she had read cover to cover, including the New Testament.

In her twenty-five years of living on Hutchison Street, she had managed to elicit some smiles from very young children who had not yet been indoctrinated. But Willa was still hopeful that one day a Hasidic man or woman would smile at her or at least smile back. Some people would have dismissed Willa as simple-minded, but that was far from the truth. Willa was a good person and full of hope. Goodness and hope defined her every bit as much as the colour of her skin. Her life would not have been possible without goodness and hope – and her smile. Not only would it have been difficult for her to live life to the fullest, but it would not have been her life. For Willa, hoping did not mean believing that everything would turn out well, but rather that everything meant something.

Willa Coleridge was twenty-three years old and had three children when she came to the neighbourhood with her parents. Her husband had left her. Actually, her husband had never lived with her. Not entirely. She was still living at home when her first child was born. The second and third were born before she was married. Then there was a church wedding, an exchange of vows and rings, a white wedding gown and a reception, although they did not share a home. The plan to live together was always postponed for financial reasons or some other excuse her husband would make up, which the young bride always fell for. Willa was gullible, like every woman in love. The last reason he gave for not living with her – the real reason – was that he was already living with another woman.

Willa lost her smile for three months, one month for each child. She had lost her lover and her children had lost their father. She had seen, seen with her very own eyes, another woman walking arm-in-arm with her husband. She had seen their children, one of whom he was proudly carrying in his arms, and another one was running up ahead. What she saw tore her guts apart. She held back her tears, she did not run away and she did not drop dead on the spot. Her children saved her. The children waved casually at their father, calling out "Hi Dad," and they kept on walking beside their mother. Their mother, Big Willa. Her children have always considered her the tallest, the most understanding, the most beautiful and the nicest mother in the world.

Willa's children were wise beyond their years. They would say: our father is our father, he is what he is. They never waited at the door clutching a suitcase. His absence didn't make them suffer or shed tears. Unlike their mother, they had no hope. They weren't unhappy children, far from it. They were just accepting and realistic. They understood that their father had sired them, end of story. When he came to see them, they were pleased, nothing more. When he left again, they picked up where they had left off, living their life with their mother and grandparents.

In the end, Willa understood her husband and she forgave him. And she forgot about him. She had a few lovers and men she could go dancing with. She even went out alone to dance at Keur Samba, a club close to where she lived. It was an inexpensive bar on Park Avenue, where a single woman could go and dance as much as she liked without having anyone hit on her. She could dance to African or Caribbean music, without even having to buy a drink, which was just perfect for her, since she didn't have much money and she liked to dance, not drink.

Spirituality moved her as much as dancing did. She was a believer. She believed in a divine force, in divine goodness. She attended church regularly. She sometimes changed churches, but never Gods. As far as she was concerned, the God of the Jews was the same as the God of the Christians or the Muslims. She would have liked to go pray one day in a mosque or a synagogue, but she didn't know how to go about it. Would they throw her out because of the colour of her skin or for some totally other reason?

Willa did not understand why some people were intolerant of their fellow human beings. She believed that people were meant to learn to love one another. Since she had experienced intolerance, rejection and even racism, on more than one occasion, she was careful not to fall into the same trap. In any case, it was not in her nature. When it came to the Jews who lived on her street, she felt bad for them rather than intolerant. She would have liked to get to know them. She thought they could give her answers to some of the questions that troubled her. She knew they were as religious as she was and she wanted to learn from them. Their children were clean and well behaved; they didn't smile, but they were polite. They almost never squabbled. They listened to their parents and the older children looked after the little ones. And it was beautiful to see how kind and respectful they were to their grandparents. Her own children were grown up now, but there would be grandchildren soon and Grandma Willa would be there for them just as her mother had been there for her and her kids. Willa wanted to learn, to know more and more, and she was always prepared to open her eyes and her heart. But she didn't know how to break through the wall behind which the Hasidim had retreated.

Her family had left Jamaica more than a hundred years ago. She didn't know much about her ancestors. She knew that her father's grandfather had worked for CN on the Halifax-Montreal line. He would toil away for more than eighteen hours a day, sleeping in a bunk on board the train. One day, when the train arrived in Montreal, he got off and never went aboard again. That's about all she knew about her family background. It wasn't for lack of interest, but she had had other fish to fry and a lot of mouths to feed. Now that her children were getting along fairly well, now that she had found a job that was not too tiring, cleaning offices downtown, her parents were dead. She didn't have anyone left to answer her questions.

When Bob Marley died, she cried, like a lot of other people did, but no more.

Montreal is her home. Hutchison Street, which connects Mile End and Outremont, is her favourite spot. In her mind, Hutchison does not separate Outremont from Mile End, as you might think; it brings them together. Willa likes to bring people together and to say good morning to her neighbours. She remembers their first names and calls out *"Comment ça va aujourd'hui"* to the francophones, or "Hello" with a smile, which never did anybody any harm. For Saint-Jean-Baptiste Day, she hangs a *fleur-de-lys* flag from her balcony and carries a smaller one to the festivities on Saint-Viateur Street. On the first of July, she gets out her Canadian flag. When there are Jewish parades and festivals, she is the first to step out onto her balcony and perhaps the only one to tap out the rhythm in time to the religious chants. She never misses a chance to celebrate, sing, or dance. Life is too short. People die young in her family, her father and mother didn't even reach the age of sixty.

It would be an understatement to say that Willa loves life. Willa *is* life. The heart, passion and smiling side of life.

She has never had enough money to go to Jamaica, although she wishes she could. Not to see the land of her ancestors, as might be expected, but because it is a country where people dance the night away. Since the Keur Samba closed its doors, she almost never goes dancing anymore. From time to time, there are parties at her church, the Church of the Apostles of Jesus Christ, but people don't dance all night.

Sometimes, on her way home from work, she hears music and sees men dancing, three houses over from hers. She stops to listen, then walks slowly up to her house, where she goes out onto the balcony. She sits outside for part of the evening, reading her Bible and listening to the chanting. On Hutchison Street, there are lots of Jewish festivals, during which people sing and dance all night.

If there were the slightest chance that they would let her in, Willa would be thrilled to go dance with her neighbours. But at the rate things are going, there is no way that will happen. Her dream of Jamaican nights is far more likely to come true than having a Hasidic family open its doors to her. She knows this, but she continues to have hope.

BENOÎT FORTIN

Benoît Fortin had rented his first apartment with his first girlfriend. It was his girlfriend who had landed the place: a 5½ she had heard about from a friend of a friend who had a friend who was leaving her cheap apartment before the lease was up because she was going on a trip. It was a real bargain, because the rent had not been increased for years. His girlfriend had convinced the landlord to let them have it without breaking the lease and jacking up the rent – *as is* – that way, he wouldn't need to repaint or do any repairs, which the place badly needed, because her boyfriend, who was very handy and a really good guy, was going to take care of everything, which he actually never did. She was super sweet, she smiled a lot. Tongue-tied and gesticulating, she finally won over the old man, whose broken English was just as bad as hers, only he had a Greek accent that was typical of the neighbourhood.

That particular girlfriend left him long ago, and others came and went like she did. But Benoît wouldn't have left his apartment for anything in the world. It was dear to his heart. It gave him stability, it was like an ID card. From one year to the next, with or without a girlfriend, he managed to cough up the rent money, which remained well below anything he could've found downtown. The landlord, who was even older now and also sick, quite simply forgot to raise the rent, and even forgot that he had a tenant who lived on the third floor.

It took Benoît fifteen minutes to get downtown by bus, on the number 80 or 160, but he was just a stone's throw from the Taverna, which had just changed its name. He lived minutes away from the Futembule, which had turned into Helm, and from all the coffee shops on Bernard, east of Park Avenue, which had sprung up overnight. It didn't take long to get to Romolo, the first café in the neighbourhood, which had grown to three times its original size, and he was one block away from Saint-Viateur Street. Ah, Saint-Viateur, on a Sunday when the sun is shining, when Café Olimpico and the Club Social are packed inside and out, with people babbling in all sorts of languages, with the aroma of coffee, crêpes and bagels in the air. Whenever he can tear himself away from his computer, Benoît likes to go there to grab a coffee, and go scouting for any pretty girls looking for guys on a sunny day made especially for chatting one another up.

From a distance, Benoît Fortin looks like a teenager. Ripped jeans, faded T-shirt, beat-up backpack, unkempt hair. He runs down the outside staircase lickety-split and walks as if he always has someone to catch up to or something pressing to do. Up close, you can see his furrowed eyebrows as he stares pleadingly from behind his patched-together eyeglasses. Without a care about his age or existential questions like "what have I done with my life?" he has reached the age of forty almost without noticing it. He is neither happy nor unhappy, and it never even occurs to him to wonder whether he is or not.

He is ecstatic just sitting at his computer, especially when he's grappling with a big problem. One day when he had just solved a gigantic problem and sent his findings to the company that hired him from time to time, he turned off his computer – it happened so rarely – and spun around in his swivel chair. He looked around the room in which he worked, he got up, he walked around the other rooms in the apartment, and he felt lonely. With his computer shut down, he felt disconnected, like the machine. Nothing, no one, had ever made him feel this way. He had never felt this empty, not even when his umpteenth girlfriend had dumped him. Not the same kind of emptiness, in any case.

Whenever one of his girlfriends left him, he had mixed feelings. He felt hurt, of course he was hurt, but, at the same time, he felt liberated. He liked living alone. According to his own rhythm, without having to worry about anyone else, without being forced to do anything he didn't want to do. That way, he could work fourteen hours in a row without having his live-in say to him, "We never do anything together, you're always working, the house is a real pigsty, and I'm pretty fed up living with a ghost."

If he knew how to resist the fairer sex, he would never live with anyone. He attracted women like flies, and he surrendered to them. He was easy prey, up to a certain point. Women could do whatever they wanted with him, but only until his work got the upper hand, until the next unsolved problem became the focus of his passion. In the days when women were less enterprising, he would have been a solitary researcher, a mad scientist whose discoveries would have come to light after his death.

He was not meant to be in a relationship. It wasn't that he didn't love women, but it was more difficult for him to find out how to make them happy, or at least content and not crabby, than it was for him to discover a hidden defect in software that someone had sent him in an emergency because they knew that he would find it. And find it he did. But he had not yet found a way to detect the flaws in his personal relationships.

Although he wasn't capable of becoming an acceptable partner, he was a generous, kind and considerate friend. When they were no longer his girlfriends, all of his exes could depend on him. Anyone could count on him to help out with any kind of problem. An aunt, brother or even cousin of one of his ex-girlfriends would have no qualms about turning to him for help. He had a very sensitive way of doing someone a favour, as if it were no trouble, and some people shamelessly took advantage of him. By getting him to fix a computer bug, to repair a bicycle, car or fridge on the blink, to babysit, or to paint a balcony.

Believe it or not, Benoît had no sense of his own value, his true value, and even if he had been aware of it, he would not have paid any attention to what he was doing or to who he was.

Benoît Fortin came from a dreary family for whom every minute of life was a burden. "A drab family," Benoît had said one day to his second girlfriend, "can we change the subject?" They weren't rich, and they weren't poor. His father worked as a foreman in a shoe factory and his mother as a nurse's aide in an old folks' home. Both of them hated their jobs, but neither would have changed jobs unless they were forced to do so. They didn't quarrel with one another, but they didn't love each other either. They lived side by side, in a lacklustre life without incident. Their three children, a girl and two boys, were docile. They didn't fight, they each had their own room, and they didn't have close ties with their parents or with one another. They would all sit down to eat at the table or in front of the television whenever their mother or father allowed them to, that was about all they did together. Around the age of fourteen or so, Benoît, the youngest, discovered computers at school. To say he felt joy or happiness would be an understatement. It was a kind of redemption. He was saved.

No one in his family had visited him in the twenty years he had lived on Hutchinson Street. No one knew where Benoît lived or even wanted to know. On several occasions, he had gone back to the suburbs where his parents lived. His brother and sister had already left home. He never thought about his childhood or teenage years, but sometimes he thought about his first computer, which miraculously appeared as a Christmas present. He was fifteen at the time.

He never had anything to say to his girlfriends or to his pals. He never said a word about the suburban neighbourhood where he had lived for more than twenty years, and he never talked about his family. But as surprising as it might seem, he would never have left of his own accord. If it hadn't been for his girlfriend, who was more bold and daring than he was and who wanted to go live in the big city at all costs, he would have stayed in that "rotten suburb," as he called it, without ever naming the exact place, when he wanted to avoid talking about it.

When he got to the city, he had the very distinct feeling of being saved for the second time in his life, this time from his past. Having found *his* place, and being free to live his *own* life. He was grateful to his first girlfriend, for whom he felt a special affection. She was the one, after all, who had served up the city to him on a silver platter, who had found this dilapidated apartment, which he loved, where he felt so much at home. Home, finally.

And to this day, even if someone gave him a castle, all expenses paid, far away from Mile End, his neighbourhood, he would never leave his 5½-room apartment on Hutchison Street.

FRANÇOISE CAMIRAND

After dreaming about the young Hasidic girl for several nights in a row, the subject of her next book came to her in a flash. She didn't have to make a conscious decision to delve into the subject. She wouldn't just put up with her dreams; instead, she would turn them to full advantage.

One morning, she got up, opened a new file and typed: Portraits of People on my Street (Tentative Title). And away she went! She always made important decisions in the morning.

Since then, she has carried out her investigations in a different way. For one of her novels in which the main character was a dancer, she had read a pile of books on dance and had attended as many dance performances as she could. But now, she doesn't know what to read or where to look. So she looks at everything. She goes for walks with her eyes and ears wide open. She goes into stores, she listens to people, she engages the shopkeepers in conversation more than she did before, and she eavesdrops on people chatting in cafés. She sits down in different parks with a book and a little notebook in her hands, waiting for something that might tickle her fancy.

She walks past the synagogue at the corner of Saint-Viateur again and again, trying to understand. She would like to slip inside through the women's entrance and attend a service. She wonders whether they would let her in, although she already knows the answer.

She reads everything she can lay her hands on about the Jewish religion, about Hasidism. She looks for works of fiction written by Hasidim, but she doesn't find much. She reads and rereads *Disobedience* by Naomi Alderman, *Lekhaim!*, the French translation of stories by Malka Zipora, *Foreskin's Lament* by Shalom Auslander, which a friend gave her, *The Street* by Mordecai Richler, and all the novels she can find by Éliette Abécassis. She consults reference books, but she keeps on looking for fiction, which will give her a better sense, she feels, of people's inner lives.

It will not be easy, she knows, to penetrate the lives of Hasidic Jews, but she will never be able to speak to the people on her street if she doesn't try to take a peek into their world. They now make up the majority of the population on Hutchison Street. In thirty-nine years, she has never crossed the threshold of a Hasidic home and she has never exchanged a single word with any of them. She has seen them. From the outside only. They are a total mystery to her.

Sometimes, the challenge she faces looms like a mountain before her. She tells herself, "They are humans, after all. Like me, like anyone, they were born and they are going to die, with obstacles between the two events. There has to be a way to catch them off guard, the way the young Hasidic girl caught me in my dream ... "

When she goes out walking, she counts the trees on the street, just for fun. She soon loses track. At the beginning of the 1980s, the sidewalk on the Mile End side of the street was widened to twice its size, and the City of Montreal planted trees all along. Some have died, but others have thrived and are still going strong. As she walks along, she hums snippets of *Pendant que*, a song by Gilles Vigneault that evokes hopes and dreams coming together and fading away again.[2] She forgets what made her start counting trees in the first place. Why not count the *mezuzot* on the doorposts of the Jewish homes instead?

In thirty-nine years, both the trees and the Hasidim have proliferated on Hutchison. Trees grow tall and *mezuzot* in flesh-coloured plastic multiply. The weather is nice today and walking has done her good. She is anxious to return to her writing. As she climbs the first few steps of her staircase, a young Hasidic boy, whom she has seen a hundred times, dashes past her.

THE DIARY OF HINDA ROCHEL

When I was little, my mother always combed my hair. I was the only girl in the family and my mother didn't have as many children as she does now. There was just my brother Yehuda and me and my mother was expecting. I had long hair. My mother brushed my hair, which she braided or sometimes tied up in a ponytail, and I liked that a lot. My brother didn't get as much attention. From time to time, my mother would shave his head and curl his sidelocks at night with a special pin, and the next morning in a split second she would unroll the payos. She spent a lot more time with me. My mother used to wear a white headscarf around the house, tied up in front with a knot at her forehead. When I was little, I thought that my mother had no hair. One day, I asked her, "Why don't you have hair like me, Mama?" "Because I shaved it off. A married woman must shave her head. Her husband must never see her hair, and no other men should either. When you grow up, you too will shave your head." "No, Mama," I exclaimed, "I don't want to cut off my hair, I don't want to look like Yehuda. I love it when you spend a long time combing my hair." I don't remember what my mother's answer was.

TAMARA

She was tall but she thought she was short, she was beautiful but she thought she was ugly, she was slim but she thought she was fat, she was good at school but she thought it was too easy. She was very talented, in a lot of ways. She had tried her hand at everything, but she had not followed through with anything. She was interested in politics, which was rare for someone of her age. Like her father did, back then, she read newspapers and anything else she could lay her hands on to keep up with current events and understand what was going on. She could carry on a conversation about the state of the world, she could analyse things, understand what worked and what didn't, but she didn't know much about her own personal state, and didn't want to know either. She attributed her malaise to the "rough patch" she was going through. She thought she would get over it, as they say, but she didn't. It persisted and even got worse.

She didn't know who she was, what she wanted, or what she was doing in this world. Life eluded her more and more. She floated between heaven and earth while waiting for someone – anyone – to tell her how to find herself and how to find some meaning in her life.

To her friends, she was the kind of person who was always on top of things, the one who had boys falling all over her, and she was the envy of all the girls. To her family, she was a distant, capricious and overly sensitive princess, hard to figure out. Anyone seeing her for the first time would be impressed by her waif-like sex appeal, her intelligence and her sense of humour, as well as the very special way she had of just scratching the surface of things, of attracting people and at the same time keeping them at a distance.

Just when her identity was the most fragile, her father disappeared without a trace. His departure was a blow to her self-esteem. She had precious little self-confidence as it was, and this event shook it to its foundation. She did not understand; she could not understand. It was a betrayal. It was beyond comprehension. Her father had abandoned her, his only daughter, his favourite child, his "little princess" as he used to call her. She realized that his love for her was nothing but a lie. My little princess, my eye! Go fuck yourself, you liar, you bastard! Her life – which had been shaped by her father's gaze – turned out to be a mere illusion. He had left without even telling her. Perhaps she would have understood why if she had known in advance. Instead, he had taken a blank sheet of paper and scribbled the words, "I can't go on living here. I am suffocating. I love you all." He had left the note on the kitchen table, addressed to no one – the coward – and signed it with his full name, first and last.

An official farewell from a traitor and gutless deserter, whom she had called Papa, Daddy, and whom she had loved and adored! She doesn't remember having cried that day, or on the days that followed. She was so hurt that the pain would have crushed her if she had not remained outside her body. Dark circles formed around her magnificent eyes. Unbeknownst to her, her home base had just been blown to bits.

Although her father had also abandoned her two brothers and her mother, she always took it as a personal affront to her. She would never forgive him for this unspeakable act, this indelible slap in the face. It brought to mind the idea of "*outrage*," a term for gross indignity that she had come across in a French play by Racine.

For years, she lied to her friends and acquaintances. She would say, "My father is dead," adding, in a simpering tone, "I am an orphan." So as not to feel the sting of those words, she would put on a coy little face. She would never have admitted that her father had abandoned her. You might as well get out your violin, while you were at it, and start bawling, adding humiliation to the indignity. Even though her father phoned from time to time or sent postcards from Hungary, New Zealand or Indonesia, the damage was already done and for her he was dead.

To release the anger and alleviate the pain, which she never talked about, not to anyone, to get through it all, she began to drink. With time, this way of coping with her anger and drowning her sorrows became a way of life.

When she was drinking, everything was fine. Everything was nicer when she was drinking. As if by magic, she felt beautiful, she became more interesting and funny, and she wasn't afraid of anything. Everything was all right, everything was there for a reason. Life, all of life, should have continued like that, pleasant and sweet, and nothing should ever have come to an end. She could finally breathe without any anxiety. She could be on the same wavelength as her friends, or her lover of the moment, and anyone else who had his eye on her. The world suddenly meant something. She was no longer alone.

She loved being drunk because it made her feel that anything was possible, that she was going to do big things in life and that she had been wrong to think that she was a nobody. She wasn't a nobody. No, she was exceptional, as her dad had so often told her. He wasn't around anymore, but it didn't matter, she was old enough to live her life without him, without her grieving mother, without her two idiot brothers. The world was magnificent, as were all the people with whom she shared the art and science of drunkenness.

She became euphoric when she thought of the world and of herself in the world in this way. It had to keep on going, on and on. Her ecstasy would grow as the evening wore on. Wine, beer and shooters. Shooters, wine and beer. Keep this high afloat, dear God, make it last forever. She was someone who had never believed in anything, but now she began to believe in a God with a white beard, in Shiva with his many comforting arms, and in carnal, spiritual and universal Love.

Then, everything began to go downhill. She never saw it coming.

How was she going to stay the course, how was she going to keep from falling off a cliff? How, indeed? Shit, shit, shit. Fuck you all. In a twinkling, it was over and she was split in two. She knew she was going too far, and at the same time, she was drawn to this extreme, bottomless pit that she knew so well, where everything was possible, in a no-holds-barred, excessive, degenerate, I'm-not-worth-any-more-than-this sense. Even though she would occasionally have a brief glimpse of what her life might be like if she "took charge of herself," an expression often bandied about, which she hated more than anything. But she had already gone too far. It was irreparable, she was sliding deeper and deeper, sliding to the death she was so afraid of, and which she craved with all her heart. Through death, she would be able to relive her childhood, be reunited with her father and mother, and become small and beautiful and joyful again. To disappear for a time, at least for a while, to get washed, to clean up, to retrieve the laugh she had had as a child and to get her big, beautiful and dreamy eyes back again. To start over again, please, please, yes, to start over again, to pick life up where she had left off, before everything had happened and conspired to make her life such a disgrace.

She's sitting by the telephone. She will never make the call that she needs to make, she knows that she will never make it, even though she knows it's an important thing for her to do. She makes up reasons for doing it, and others for not doing it. There are a lot of good reasons for picking up the phone and saying who she is and what she wants, and there are a lot of good reasons for not letting someone turn her down and reject her, "It's not the right day, it's not the right time, I don't know what to tell him, it's no use, the secretary will tell me he's in a meeting, I don't feel well enough, he won't take me, I am not good enough, I don't have any experience, why should I leave my job, I like it where I am, I'm going to stutter, I would be better off writing to him first, and anyway it's no use, he doesn't know me." She even manages to convince herself that it would be better to drop into his office instead of telephoning. But she knows she will never stop by his office, even though she's trying, at the moment, to believe that she will.

Her breathing becomes laboured. She is having an anxiety attack. Without thinking, she goes to the fridge. A beer will help her think better, yes, that's it, a beer to help her think about how to go about it.

With a very cold beer in her hand, she goes out onto the front balcony. It's nice out and the sun is shining on the Mile End side of Hutchison Street, her side. She sits down, stretches out her legs, takes a big swig of beer, puts the bottle down on the low table next to her, closes her eyes, and lets the sun wash over her face. She prays to her gods, one at a time, to tell her what to do. What to do with her life.

In her mind, she imagines herself standing in front of the telephone with indescribable anxiety pressing down on her chest. She is ashamed of herself. A telephone, a trivial little telephone. What is preventing me from moving forward, what is stopping me? She takes another mouthful, puts the cold bottle between her two small breasts, pushes hard against her solar plexus until it hurts. She waits, with her eyes closed.

In this particular instance, just saying "this is who I am, this is what I want" is as dangerous for Tamara as jumping out of an airplane without a parachute. When the time comes to make the last ditch effort to assert herself, to face up to her fears, to stand on her own two feet, she goes to get herself a beer, then a second one, and a third ... and her anxieties vanish.

She has always been the kind of person that people look at, coddle, admire, and choose. A modern version of Sleeping Beauty. Living her life on a pedestal, up above the ground, she had avoided grappling with her problems. Until now, she has managed to live life as if she were surfing through it.

Nothing satisfied her. She had a high opinion of herself, but she lacked the self-confidence and tenacity to pursue what she really wanted. She didn't even know what she wanted. She had lost her bearings, she no longer knew what she expected out of life, and even less what she expected from herself. She was no longer able to go with the flow, as she had done before, or else to spring into action to steer her life in another direction. To go for something, or someone, would involve risks she never wanted to take.

Since the disappearance of her father, and maybe even before, she had spent her life waiting. She waited for classes to end, for the boyfriend she didn't love anymore to bugger off, for another guy to notice her and to fall madly in love with her. She waited for evening to come so she could go drinking, and in the morning she waited for her head to stop aching. She waited for her boring job to be over, to get her pay cheque so she could go blow it all. She would never admit it, but she was waiting for her father to return, even though she knew that she could never forgive him, that she would hold it against him until the day he died, and that she actually wished he were dead. She was waiting for a miracle. Any old miracle that would change her life.

FRANÇOISE CAMIRAND

She flitted like a butterfly from one character to another, from her notebooks to her characters. From the street to her computer. She had files full of notes taken haphazardly as she read, as she walked around. She would grapple with one of the characters, then embrace one of the others. She was moving forward in baby steps. One word here, one sentence there. Rewrite a section, fix another, polish many ...

Sentences, ideas, emotions and images swirled around in her brain pell-mell. In the time it took to decide which character went with each of these, they vanished ... and then returned even more distinctly ... She would then put them down on paper, telling them, "wait, your time will come." By protecting them from oblivion, she felt calm, and so were they. Emotions can wait until we arouse them.

Characters appeared and took shape.

She continued to stroll up and down Hutchison Street, from Van Horne to Mont-Royal and back. Sometimes she took Park Avenue on the way home.

Each time she goes for a walk, she sings a different song. Today she has picked *Mistral gagnant*, a nostalgic piece in which the songwriter recalls walking in the rain by the seaside with his young daughter.[3]

For a change, she decides to take the back lane behind Hutchinson. That's where she sees her. The old lady, standing on the edge of the laneway, is calling to the birds, concentrating so hard that it looks like this is the most important thing in the world.

Françoise has seen her in the neighbourhood hundreds of times, and although the old woman lives only four doors down, she has never seen her in action, in her own world.

Françoise remains hidden behind the fence and watches her for a long time. She hears her chirping well before she hears the birds. When they dive frantically to snatch bits of torn-up bread, the old lady's face lights up with a breathtaking smile. She has the disarming look and movements of a happy little girl. As if her smile and innocent gestures alone could make the universe come to life.

Both laughable and dignified, this moment encapsulates all that is laughable and dignified in our world …

THÉRÈSE HUOT

She didn't get this thing about loving your neighbour. At school, they had filled her head with the words of Jesus Christ. His famous line "Thou shalt love thy neighbour as thyself" popped up more often than it deserved to. But it really didn't mean anything to her. Thérèse Huot loved animals, and had always preferred them to humans. It didn't sort itself out as she grew older either. Even now, with the exception of kids under five, she far preferred cats, birds, all animals without exception. She didn't discriminate against any kind of animal, whether it was beautiful, ugly, old, injured, sick, flea-ridden, jumpy, thieving or aggressive. She even liked the weaker ones, the ones who weren't able to fend for themselves. Each and every one of them had a right to her attention, to her affection, to her food, to her water, to her caring and stroking. The animals who hung around the Hutchison Street alley could sense that about her, and they knew where to go in case of need. They would even drop by, just like that, to greet the others, and to lick the kind and generous hands of their hostess.

After her husband died and her children disappeared,

the old lady befriended the lonely and the hungry, but she lived alone. So there was no one left to tell her that she was going way too far, all that food costs a pile of money in the long run, and what good does it do, can you tell me that, with nothing to show for it but all that stinking shit to pick up, but go for it, if you like to work for nothing and throw your money out the window, that's what I think anyways ... Finally, she could live in peace ... peace and quiet.

She never invited anyone over to her place except cats and dogs. The squirrels invited themselves over and, with an abundant supply of all kinds of seeds, the birds made permanent nests there. Most of the time, her visitors stayed in the yard and lounged around under the only tree she had, a Manitoba maple. She would go from one to the other, talking to them, stroking them, giving them something to eat or drink. She would sit down with them on the indestructible plastic chair she kept out there year round. In the winter, the balcony was a place where her guests could be more comfortable, and the kitchen was even better on very frosty nights.

Thérèse Huot never used the front door to go outside. She went out through the back and took the alley which was a few steps away from Park Avenue. Even in winter, she always managed to beat a path through the snow drifts, even though she ran the risk of hurting her back. The alley was an extension of her backyard, and she felt at home there, despite the garbage and the truck traffic which made it dangerous to walk. But she would do anything to discover an animal she didn't know yet, and to crumble a few slices of the bread she always had stashed in her handbag, while making strange noises that attracted the birds and amused the truck drivers.

If the residents of Hutchison Street had seen her walking in their street, they would have mistaken her for a homeless person gone astray. Hutchison was not an elegant street. It was populated by all sorts of people and more and more Hasidim, but there were never any bums, vagrants or beggars. Those people usually kept to Park Avenue, where they would stand in front of the Dollarama, the Jean-Coutu drugstore or the SAQ liquor store with a paper coffee cup in their hand and all their worldly goods crammed into a battered suitcase on wheels. Each one had a different way of panhandling, of getting your attention, of saying thank you or uttering some other cliché, or of smiling to make you feel sorry for them as you went past. The regulars who did their shopping on Park Avenue knew them all by heart. Mysteriously, the donors and recipients selected one another. You ended up giving a few coins to your favourite, and you neglected others without even feeling guilty about it. Allah is great and God is just, someone else would look after those ones.

On Saturdays, and sometimes Sundays, there was a particular beggar who pitched up in the neighbourhood. She was not like the others. She would always stand in the same place, not in a doorway, but between Mile End Grocery and the drugstore, back from the sidewalk, winter and summer, all day long. She wore clean clothes, she sported an imitation leather shoulder bag, her feet were firmly placed on the ground, and she stared straight out in front of her, motionless, without asking for anything, her hands clutching her coffee cup which she held tightly against her chest. She would stretch out her hand whenever anyone was about to offer her a coin, but then she would pull it back right away. In the winter, even after a helluva snowfall, when it was friggin' cold out, she didn't stamp her feet. She remained rooted there, always standing tall on a flattened cardboard box that she brought along to protect herself from the cold.

Thérèse Huot, too, had chosen her pet. She first saw the newcomer on a Saturday, wearing a fuchsia-coloured hat with a big pin on it in the shape of a cat. Thérèse came up and stood beside her, so as not to get in the way of any potential donors, and she asked her if she liked cats. And that did it! Every Saturday they picked up their conversation where they had left off the previous week. Cats, health, children, money, the cold, the heat – there were plenty of subjects for a good chinwag every week on the way to the stores and back again. After all, they saw each other only once a week. Madame Huot sometimes brought cookies she had picked up at Dollarama, her favourite store, along with a thermos she had also picked up at the dollar store and which she had filled to the brim with very hot and very sweet tea. She held on to the paper coffee cup while Madame Groulx was eating and drinking.

The image of these two women was disconcerting:

standing next to one another, cup in hand, they chatted and chuckled while peering at the passersby. With their old-fashioned hats and eccentric way of dressing, they looked like two clowns who were making fun of other people, or else two panhandlers. And if they were begging, what on earth was so funny?

For those who regularly came to do their shopping on Park Avenue, the Saturday beggar was the Saturday beggar. But for Thérèse Huot, she became Madame Groulx, the only human being she had talked to since her husband died, not counting the few sentences she exchanged with shopkeepers or the two or three words she used to tell her neighbour to go to hell when she tried to preach to her about having too many animals in her yard.

Thérèse Huot had never dropped coins into Madame Groulx's cup, except for the first time, before she knew her. Not because she was stingy, but because she was embarrassed. They had become friends, and a loony tossed quickly into the coffee cup was worth nothing compared to the three and a half years of delightful chatter in good weather and in bad.

Thérèse Huot did not have a lot of money, but she felt rich because she lived her life exactly the way she wanted. Henri, her husband, had had only one good idea in his life: to buy the apartment where they lived. Apart from maintenance, taxes and other annoyances, it didn't cost her anything to live there anymore. "I am a fat cat," she reminded herself often. Her late husband's pension and her old age pension were more than enough for her to feed herself and spoil all the critters who paid her a visit, to make donations to two organizations that protected animals, and to visit the Granby Zoo twice a year. Thérèse had worn the same beige raincoat in spring, summer, and fall for at least thirty years, and a brown winter coat with a fur collar that was timeworn and definitely moth-eaten. She had no needs, none whatsoever, and she couldn't give a damn about the people who stared at her. As long as there were little creatures who came to see her, she was happy. And there were animals in the alley behind Hutchison Street alright, not counting her cats, Duchess, Tartine and Cavaleur, and her dog, Caboche.

Her children also dropped by from time to time. She would open her door to them whenever they popped in, but she didn't much care one way or the other. Even though she had a preference for animals and pre-school children, and was not naturally drawn to adult human beings, she didn't hate them either. "They're my children, after all!" But she no longer had anything in common with them and the way they lived their lives. They bought and sold all kinds of things that were a mystery to her, they squirreled their money away in banks, and they acted super important. They came to visit her as if they were doing her a favour or as if they were doing their semi-annual good deed. Fine, they didn't stay long. All three of them would roll in at the same time, more to meet one another than to see her. They talked about their affairs — it was all Greek to her — about their latest purchases, sailboats, cars and houses. She would never see any of that stuff, but in any case she didn't give a shit.

If they ever brought their babies, that would be different. But she knew that would never happen. Her kids didn't like animals or babies either. Too bad, because their mother, Thérèse Huot, happened to prefer babies who cry or laugh, birds who chirp, cats who meow, purr or lap up their milk, all animals, actually, except squirrels. She had never seen animals collect things and stash them away in a bank, except squirrels ... and her children.

FRANÇOISE CAMIRAND

She hadn't invited anyone over for dinner in a long time. In the evening, she would often eat with Jean-Hugues, her lover, who was also her publisher. She preferred to have her three writer friends over, without him. He knew it. And even before she reminded him, he would steal away, alleging that he had a deadline to meet or an important meeting to attend, so he wouldn't be insulted at not having been invited.

She had decided to make *kapama* for them, with marinated chicken. It was not a fancy dish, but it took a very long time to prepare.

She had discovered *kapama* on a trip to Bulgaria she had made long before. Her host, Madam Gabrovo, had taught her how to stuff vine leaves with meat and rice, although instead of looking like neat little cigars, her *sarmi* were shapeless and bulgy and looked like they would pop open when they were cooked. Madam Gabrovo would take one out of her hands and deftly whip the disgraceful lump into an elegantly folded vine leaf. "You have to practise, Françoise. I've rolled thousands of these, and you haven't even done ten. It takes patience." Françoise learned how, in the end.

Madam Gabrovo used to prepare the dish on special occasions only, except that when she saw how much Françoise loved *kapama*, she couldn't resist making it more frequently, if only to witness her guest's pleasure. And, who knows, maybe she would even end up learning to roll acceptable vine leaves. What's more, Madam Gabrovo thought it was amazing to host a Québec novelist. She was particularly proud of it since she had read and appreciated all of her work and was planning to translate her latest novel.

Every time that Françoise made *kapama* — which she, too, did only on special occasions — she remembered Madam Gabrovo and her laugh, her charming accent and her impeccable French. "Françoise, everything is in the breathing. That's what people here say. What distinguishes one dish from another, even when they have basically the same ingredients, is the way the cook breathes. It makes all the difference and gives the dish a unique taste ... Just like in a novel," she added with a complicit smile.

Each time, Françoise would bring out the yellowed piece of paper on which she had written the recipe. She would read it over again, even though she knew it by heart.

Rub the chicken pieces with salt, then rinse under running water and drain. Marinate in olive oil, garlic, lemon juice and spices for at least twenty-four hours. Cover the bottom of a earthenware casserole with plain vine leaves, then place the chicken pieces on the vine leaves leaving as little space between the pieces as possible. Arrange the stuffed *sarmi* on top of the chicken, placing each one tightly against the other, in several layers if necessary, and sprinkle with a few cloves of garlic. Cover with an over-turned plate. Then fill the pot, three-quarters full, with homemade chicken stock, or else water with a bit of salt. Cover and bring the mixture to the boiling point, then let it simmer slowly. Taste it to see whether it's cooked, but don't eat it all up. Save some for your guests. Serve with yoghurt flavoured with dried mint leaves.

She prepared the meal in several stages. When she wasn't able to write anymore, when her characters eluded her, she would roll a few *sarmi* and freeze them.

With each vine leaf that she rolled – with just the right amount of meat and rice, not too much or else the roll would be less juicy, not too little, because it would lose its shape and the taste of the leaf would overpower the taste of the filling – Françoise would think about her friends. She would imagine the evening unfolding ... what her friends would talk about, the distinct way each of them would talk, listen, laugh and make the others laugh. It was fun. She enjoyed the evening in advance. Making food for a dinner party was like writing a book. Everything happens beforehand, first in the imagination, then in reality, when you put the rice on to cook, when you prepare the meat, the same way a word turns into a sentence, and a character turns into a story. Everything is carefully arranged so that the guests (or the readers) can relish it the way you thought they would. After all, a meal is merely a pretext for getting together and enjoying the company of your friends – just like a book.

Her friends had started to write at nearly the same time she did. They didn't know each other when they published their first book, but, gradually, they met at literary gatherings, found they had things in common, and became friends. Two at a time at first, then all four of them. They were young, they saw each other often, they read each other's writing, they gave each other feedback and they were supportive of each other. They each liked what the others wrote. There was no jealousy among them. At certain times, one of them would be successful, while another was struggling; at other times, the opposite would happen. Despite the ups and downs, they all continued to respect and admire everyone's writing. Even when it became a challenge to find an evening when all four of them were free at the same time, their friendship endured, as strong as ever.

They would laugh, they would gab, they would chitter-chatter. They talked about everything and nothing. Then, each of them would speak at length while the others listened. They would each take a turn, and speak as long as they wanted about their writing, where they were at, sometimes raising a particular writing problem they were having, which the others discussed with enthusiasm and generosity.

One of them was writing a play based on her trip to Africa, the other was working on something set in China, and the third was doing a screenplay for a feature film taking place between Chibougamau and the North Pole. Françoise was the only person who hadn't ventured one inch beyond the confines of her hometown.

She told them about her project, now well underway, to write a novel based on the characters of Hutchison Street. "Why Hutchison?" they asked. "Because I've been living here since the age of sixteen," she replied, "and this is the first time that I'll be talking about the people I've been bumping into on my street all these years."

And she began to tell them what was special about Hutchison and the people who lived there.

She had seen her neighbours walking, each one in a characteristic manner that was recognizable, even from a distance. She had seen them talking to the shopkeepers, to the cashiers, and to each other. She had seen them ambling down the aisles of the Four Brothers store, dawdling over an array of products at the drugstore, shifting from foot to foot impatiently as they waited in line at the cash, or reading a mystery book while waiting for their prescriptions to be ready. At the Y, she had sometimes seen people without their clothes on although she didn't even know what their name was.

She had heard them speaking French, English, Yiddish, Greek, Arabic, Armenian, Italian, Chinese and other languages she didn't recognize. She had heard francophones speaking English, sometimes to be polite, or sometimes because they were too lazy to repeat what they had just said, or to speak slowly enough to be understood, or sometimes also because they were self-effacing or lacked self-confidence. She had heard the people who came from other countries ask these same francophones, "Why are you speaking to me in English? Because I look like a foreigner, is that it? You Québécois, you make me die laughing. Make up your mind, once and for all!"

She had seen then cleaning up their yards, watering their gardens, feeding the birds, obediently waiting in line at the bank, or else jumping the queue to get ahead of somebody else. She had seen them waiting at the bus stop, shivering, humming to themselves, crying. She had seen them sitting on their balconies, alone or with friends, digging their cars out of a snowbank and cursing, or else lending someone else a hand. She had watched them give spare change to a street person, shop for fruit, get out of a taxi, leave a grocery store, yell at the store keeper or joke around with him, take the time to pick out a fine wine or else grab the first bottle they laid their hands on. She had seen them in the parks of Outremont and in the cafés of Mile End. She had heard the Hasidim chanting as she strolled past their open windows and gangs of kids singing together.

She had seen them so many times in thirty-nine years.

She had seen women in slippers, wearing a black or white turban and a big winter coat that was partly open, surrounded by children who were all bundled up, waiting in the bitter cold for the school bus that seemed to take forever to come. She had seen them pushing their double strollers, with a long line of other children walking after them.

She had seen Hasidic couples staring at one another lovingly, boys on bicycles racing down the sidewalk, little ones holding on to the pant legs of their brothers and the skirts of their sisters, babies in their fathers' arms, teenagers stepping out arm-in-arm with grandmothers who could barely walk.

She had seen boys and girls carrying parcels for their old neighbours who needed a cane or walker to get around. She had seen actresses she knew from television or the theatre, whom no one else recognized.

She had seen girls and boys staggering home at four o'clock in the morning, the very ones she had once seen as babies, and who were now having some of their own.

She had seen people make fun of the Hasidim and laugh at them to their face or behind their back. More than once, she had seen a man smiling maliciously as he sicced his big dog on Jewish children knowing full well that they have an atavistic fear of animals and especially dogs.

She had seen ambulances, houses on fire, police cars, funeral processions with her neighbours in tears, grief-struck and unable to find their way home.

She had seen *yeshivot* and synagogues under construction, *sukkot* set up on balconies and *mikva'ot* tucked into basements.

She had seen Hasidic processions, and Greek weddings, and, at the time of the referendum on Quebec independence, signs saying "*Oui*" and others "*Non, merci.*"

She had seen marital squabbles, fights between friends, disputes between neighbours.

She had seen people at their windows, looking out at the street out of boredom while other people were on the outside looking in, trying to see what was going on behind the windows.

"I have been seeing all this since the age of sixteen. Sometimes, without looking. It's crazy what you can see when you're not paying attention. We can't help it — by looking, the foreign becomes familiar with the passage of time."

"I have always wanted to be a bird, or else an invisible camera, a camera that doesn't make any noise, that can penetrate a person's heart to discover how it beats when no one is watching it. Voyeurs like to look at forbidden acts, whereas I like hidden feelings. Inner feelings. What a person is experiencing deep inside and with the people she loves or does not love. I like to hear what's simmering inside a person. Whatever they are unable to experience. Whatever is stagnant. I want to understand how, and by which process, a person has become the way she is. And why she did not become what she should have become. Or what she would have liked to be. I have always wanted to be able to walk through walls … to penetrate the walls that people build around themselves."

She got up to get the dessert, to bring fresh glasses and plates, and open another bottle of wine. They raised a glass to the joy of being together and, after taking another gulp of wine, she carried on.

"The word 'fraternal' is perhaps a bit strong, but that's what I feel when I'm writing about my neighbours … I fraternize with them … even though they are not necessarily aware of it, and even though my fondness for them will remain unrequited. It doesn't matter. It's just such a pleasure for me to get nearer to them, to capture the fleeting moments when I have watched them and put them into words. I would like to spin an invisible web extending from me to them, from them to me. I would like to be able to touch the part of them that resides in me. And perhaps — why not? — that part of me that resides in them."

She stopped abruptly and blushed. "Oh, my god. If I have been looking at them and seeing them for so many years, it means that they, too, have been watching me and seeing me."

"Don't worry," her friend laughed. "No one on your street is going to write a book about you, except your biographer perhaps. But you would have to have one foot in the grave already, which is not going to happen anytime soon."

So they drank to her health and to the health of her prospective biographer. And the discussion continued. The way in which writers look at society, then the people on her block, and, of course, the Hasidim — oh my, how are you going to do it? They went on, asking one question after another.

The evening was coming to a close. Everyone thought it had been great fun, the *kapama* had been delicious, and enough to feed an army. The only guy in the group, who was also the only one with children who still lived at home, was happy to bring home a plateful of *sarmi* and chicken, which would be a real treat for his kids. "Or else," he said with a chuckle, "I could volunteer to eat some more, as usual."

She was happy to have seen her friends, and tired, as well. She had not talked this much since her last media tour.

All of their questions and comments were buzzing about in her head, and she was anxious to go to bed, to sleep, and to wake up rested so she could begin working again.

ALAIN PASQUIER

Alain Pasquier had been living in his large 8½-room apartment on Hutchison Street for over thirty years. Over time, his home had filled up with furniture, objects, gizmos, thingamajigs, thick file folders overflowing with yellowed papers, and cabinets and bookcases crammed full of stuff. Paintings, posters and photos covered every square inch of the walls. His closets were bursting at the seams with big green garbage bags and beat-up suitcases that his children were going to pick up — I swear I will, Dad — just as soon as they found a bigger place to live. For some time now, the apartment had been covered with a thick coat of dust, which is not very *feng shui*, they say, because dust is a sign of death.

Alain and Marie-Claude, his first wife, had bought the apartment for fifteen thousand dollars at the end of the 1970s. They had found it expensive at the time, and would not have been able to buy it if Marie-Claude's kind and rich aunt hadn't died and given them a head start. They were both young part-time university teachers. She taught mathematics and he taught literature. Life was beautiful.

Looking at his downcast and disillusioned face now, you could scarcely believe that he had once been happy. Had he really? A man of Pasquier's age has every right to wonder. When he was living with Marie-Claude he didn't have time for soul-searching questions like am I happy, do I like teaching, do I want to have children, haven't I wanted to be a writer since the age of twelve? His wife was a rather effective blend of a bulldozer and a nightingale, whereas he was indecisive and totally lacking in self-confidence. The bulldozer took charge when Alain was undecided and the nightingale smoothed over his lack of self-confidence. He was crazy about her, and her love for him would have saved the world, if the world and Alain could have been saved. Two children were born of their union and in this home.

You might think that he had failed to fulfil his dreams, and that was why he had such a shrivelled up and miserable look about him as he walked along Hutchison or anywhere else, that he had been defeated, like many others, by the hurly-burly of day-to-day life – work, kids, I make a good living so why should I worry about my lot in life, why would I wish for anything else? But, truth be told, he had never had any dreams. He had suppressed any dreams the minute they threatened to sneak through the backdoor of his consciousness. He had every right to whine, to be disgruntled, to resent the entire world, but he had not allowed himself to dream.

Alain was not fully aware of who he was. Any ideas or

feelings he had about himself were amorphous or inconsistent. He would consider himself highly intelligent one day, but the following day or even an hour later, he would think he was the most stupid and incompetent good-for-nothing. He was neither exceptional nor useless. Like seven-eighths of the world population, in fact, he fell somewhere in between the two extremes. But being average was of no interest to him. He preferred to think of himself as either superior or else bloody stupid. He was fifty-five years old, but it had never occurred to him to question the two opposite positions he had taken since childhood. It's hard to break long-standing habits we adopt in childhood, as anyone who has grappled with them in therapy or other forms of soul-searching would tell you. Several times a day, Alain Pasquier fluctuated between vanity and humility, like a balloon that was inflated and deflated. A simple smile from one of his female students would get him pumped, just as a single word of criticism could upset him and knock him off his feet until the next benevolent look or kind word perked him up again.

In love or not, loved or not, he was never relaxed, calm, happy, self-assured. He was never worry-free. He was a troubled person, carrying a burden without understanding its nature and cause. He would smile and sometimes laugh, but his smile bore the traces of deep-rooted pain and his laugh, often tinged with bitterness, was joyless.

Alain Pasquier did not know who he was, but it didn't matter to him. What he wanted, what he desired most in the world — and this was perhaps the driving force in his whole life – was to be loved by the woman he loved. Without the loving gaze of a woman, cracks would appear in the mirror in which he saw his reflection. His life would go off the rails, even though, when you thought about it, his life had never been completely on track from childhood on.

Alain Pasquier had always had a way with women. If you saw him slumped in his armchair, his eyes red from crying, you would wonder what women could possibly have seen in him. Oh, he has charm, a lot of charm. There's something in his beautiful sad eyes and in his whole being that begs for salvation. Or, in a more poetic vein, he is saying, I am placing my head, my heart, my entire body in your beautiful white hands. Crush me, if you feel like it, without you I am nothing. Naturally, any woman who was the least bit maternal or romantic or who had the mettle of Jesus Christ our Saviour, or a female version thereof, would become entrapped by his beautiful misty eyes and his romantic poet's mane of hair.

His lovers and his two legal wives were never disappointed, at least in one respect: Alain Pasquier was an exceptional lover. He loved women, womankind, femininity – except his mother and sisters, whom he loathed with a guilty passion.

He adored the company of women, their conversation, their interests, their concerns, their intelligence, their boundless capacity for love, their good nature, and the mood swings brought on by their menstrual cycles, whims or the simple need to be true to their feelings.

He had no interest in talking about hockey, cars, or the ups and downs of the stock market. He far preferred what the Brits would refer to as small talk over a cup of tea, gossip, and (yes!) shopping, going to the theatre, and, of course, reading books – popular novels as well as the classics from Duras to Yourcenar, from Proust to Fuentes and Vásquez Montalbán, authors he had introduced them to and taught them to appreciate. All of his friends were women, with the exception of one childhood friend he still had dinner with once or twice a year, which was just enough to remind him that the company of men meant little to him, and what would I do, dear God, if from one day to the next, there were no more women in the world?

Once he got over them, he would get in touch with them again, and they would come back, having forgotten the terrible scenes, the foul language, the lies, the blackmail and the insulting letters. He had charm, all right, and women liked his company as much as he liked theirs. His former students, who had got a lot from their professor, would reappear years later. Pasquier was generous with his time and knowledge. He was never condescending. He was always stimulating and his classes were full. No matter whether he was depressed, discouraged or disappointed in life, he always gave it his all when he walked into class and he taught brilliantly.

Alain Pasquier had always been incapable of looking ahead, of seeing himself in the future, but he could relive the past at will, down to the slightest detail, especially the things that had been painful.

Of all the women who had dumped him, his first big love, the mother of his children, still took the prize for the length and intensity of suffering she had caused when they separated. Depression, one year on sick leave. At the time, his mother, who had never loved him, had none-theless come to look after him. Marie-Claude had walked out on him, leaving him the house and kids, and bye-bye, I don't want to have anything more to do with you. He had fallen into the depths of despair, particularly since Marie-Claude had been ruthless. After having told him clearly why she was leaving, she had disappeared. Disap-peared without a trace. She had given him back his life by loving him and, with one fell swoop, she had pulled the plug. Complete darkness. Nothingness. As if nothing had ever existed between them. As if he had never existed. He no longer had a grip on life. Everything collapsed. No floor, no ceiling. Only an old crevice into which he had fallen. He was disappearing into his childhood malaise, and reliving his own lack of life – if you can call such horror living.

He felt more or less the same kind of pain each time he went through a separation. "Why do they all leave me? I love them so much. I have loved them so much. I can't live without them. I have done everything. I have done everything …"

His second wife has just walked out on him. "Oh God, I want to die …"

She has been speaking for a long time. He hasn't heard anything, but he knows. It is final and there is no going back. He will never get over it. He is too old. Broken. At the end of his tether. An old dirty sock with holes in it, buried at the bottom of the laundry hamper. Life doesn't mean anything anymore, it never has.

She is going down the stairs. "I am worth nothing because she doesn't love me."

He hears the front door close.

He falls to pieces completely. I am worth nothing because she doesn't love me, a refrain recorded at the age of five, when he was absolutely sure that his mother would never love him. Sounds are amplified and distorted. "I am worth nothing. I'm a failure. My life has never amounted to much. I will die the way I was born. Rejected. A beggar. Even my mother. All my life, I have begged. Love me. Even my children love their mother more than me. I, too, loved my mother ... Just a smile, a kind look ... God, how I loved her. God, how I loved her. I am tired. Tired."

Alain Pasquier's daughter was in the habit of coming to see her father once a week. Actually, she came to do her laundry. That day, she found him asleep. It's really unusual for him to be asleep on the living room couch, she thought at first.

She didn't notice the handwritten note lying on the floor between the coffee table and the couch.

There were lots of papers lying all over the apartment. Two dressers and four desks overflowing with file folders and piles of papers held down by paper weights in all shapes and sizes. Her father had a lot of projects on the go, some begun long ago, none of which had ever been completed. But he kept the paperwork handy, close by, just in case ...

THE DIARY OF HINDA ROCHEL

My cousin Avrami just came from New York. Our whole house has changed. I'm just happy to be going to school. Even on Shabbat, which is my favourite day because there is peace in the home, it's not the same anymore. Everything is spoiled because of him. He doesn't want to go to the *yeshiva* with my brother. And I don't know what part of the house to go to anymore. I can't stay locked up in the bathroom all day. He's always moving around. He changes his clothes several time a day, he goes out, he comes back in, he goes out again, and he comes back right away. He never touches the *mezuzah*, not when he goes out, and not when he comes back in. He doesn't give a hoot whether our house is blessed or not. He wants to drive my father's car. "May God forgive you, Avrami, you know perfectly well that it's Shabbat." Avrami then said some bad words that I can't write down. My mother burst into tears and my father, who is usually so gentle, had to control himself so that he wouldn't slap him. I wanted to ask my father why Avrami had come to live with us. But I didn't dare. Things were going so badly. Good bye *shalom bayit*. Peace in the home has gone out the window. Even our Shabbat meal wasn't good, in spite of all the candles we lit and all the good things there were to eat.

Perhaps it was good, but I couldn't taste anything. My brother went to the *yeshiva* anyway to sing and pray. If there had been a *yeshiva* for girls, I would have rushed over there, too.

Usually, we sing during the Shabbat meal and even afterward. But Avrami spoiled everything. Even the younger kids were on edge. They didn't have their beautiful Shabbat faces on. Even they got yelled at.

My father always says, "We don't sing because we are happy, we are happy because we sing." But this time, nothing. We didn't sing. When Avrami left, Papa was agitated, emotional, I think. "*Oy vey! Oy vey!* I feel sorry for my brother, having a son like Avrami," he said. "I don't know what he's going to do, may God help him." Usually, it's my mother who says "*Oy vey! Oy vey!*" Not my father.

I went out into the backyard, and my little brothers followed me. I would have liked to be by myself to think about all that. But since it was not possible, I started to think about how I would translate "*Oy vey!*" into French for my diary. I came up with the French expression, "*quel malheur.*" There's a lot of *malheur*, or misfortune, in Gabrielle Roy's book, too. Just thinking about her main character, Florentine, I felt a little less sad.

FRANÇOISE CAMIRAND

There's nothing more touching than walking along Hutchison Street on a Saturday and seeing entire Hasidic families all dressed up in their "Shabbat best." They are all out in their finery, from the smallest child to the biggest one, including the spectacular *shtreimel*. It conjures up images of Sunday mass, for those who are old enough to remember, when people would gather on the steps of churches throughout Quebec. This occurred in the 1950s, and even into the early 1960s, when Françoise still went to church with her mother, father, sister and brothers, all of them dressed up from head to toe in their Sunday best. The worst thing about it was that they had to stay clean and well behaved all day. Françoise was allowed to read. Her school teacher would let her take a few books home for the weekend. Once she had devoured them, she would read them to her sister.

She passes a family of ten, including the parents. There are two babies in a double stroller, two little girls between four and six who are dressed alike in identical new bonnets and long satin dresses. They scamper along, pleased with how they look, showing off their new patent-leather shoes. Hasidic or not, a new pair of shoes is always an important event for a child. Two eighteen-year-old boys, miniature men, proudly sport a suit and tie, a freshly laundered white shirt and a holiday *kippah*. They are running up ahead. The parents lag behind, with their two teenaged girls, also dressed the same, except that their beautiful, clean and shiny hair is done in a slightly different way.

As she goes home, she is thinking about all the work the mothers do. Shabbat waits for no one. It arrives at a set time, once a week. Everything needs to be ready before they can light the Shabbat candles. To observe the compulsory period of rest, a mother needs to work like crazy in the days leading up to the Sabbath. She has to see to all the little details, follow all the religious guidelines and, above all, remember everything. The closer the time comes, the more the pressure builds. There are suits to clean, white shirts to wash and iron, three meals to prepare, bread dough to knead, groceries to buy, treats to get for the children — because it's Shabbat, and everything needs to be taken care of so that there's nothing left to do during this blessed day of rest, for the glory of the All-Powerful. And, above all, the mothers must not forget to set the timer, which enables the cooking to start and stop on time, without anyone's intervention. Every week, mothers struggle to get everything done right down to the minute. If someone forgets to set the all-important timer, no food. You could rely on the grandmother, perhaps, who doesn't live too far away. But has she prepared a meal for twelve?

Fifty-two Shabbats a year, in addition to countless other holidays, each with their specific set of strict rules, to be adhered to in all cases. Orthodox or Hasidic mothers will be the first to ascend to heaven on the wing of an eagle. There's no doubt about it. If not, is there any divine justice?

HERSHEY ROZENFELD

Scorned by everyone, considered an oddball and a good-for-nothing, Hershey Rozenfeld was the laughingstock of the community. Instead of singling him out as someone who was setting a bad example, people preferred to ridicule him and ostracize him that way. Would any child or teenager look up to a ridiculous man whom everyone made fun of?

Some good souls were more than willing to tell him to go back to where he came from. In New York, at least, he would be far away, and good riddance, our children don't need bad examples. The community doesn't need dead wood or another rotten apple either, there are already enough hatless men around, although you can't do anything about those people, since they have been living in the neighbourhood longer than we have. The only thing we can do is not look at them.

Righteous folks were irritated and shocked by the fact that he talked to Goys or *Goyim*, to use the more precise Jewish term for the Gentiles. He even let some of them set foot in his home, where they would drink a cup of coffee or even a glass of beer with him. What a scandal!

In order to move out of his uncle's house, Hershey Rozenfeld married a sickly girl whom nobody wanted. The young bride died shortly thereafter, even before bearing a child. That was fine with him, he didn't really want offspring – something that his fellow Hasidim would consider heresy.

After his mother died – he was just eleven years old – his father had sent him to live in Montreal with his uncle. He had never felt at home with his new family, or in his new community. He was a Hasidic Jew, and he believed in God, but he wasn't really devout, and he didn't want to pretend that he was. He didn't like groups, and he was even more averse to being part of a group. He retreated into himself so that people would leave him alone, and would forget about him. Most of the time, it worked.

He did everything differently from everyone else.

He treasured the lessons he had learned from his mother. "My son," she had told him not long before she died, "there are good men and there are bad men everywhere. A *kippah* does not guarantee that someone is good. Hatless men can also be good. Don't forget that."

He had not forgotten.

He had never intended to be sacrilegious. He liked his religion, even though he found it a bit too rigid for his tastes. There were too many commandments, too many rules, too many things that were forbidden and too many prayers. You had to be careful about everything you did, about everything you looked at, about every morsel of food you ate and every drop of liquid you drank.

Everything was considered either pure or impure. Nothing in between. Everything was controlled, dictated, regulated. There were many precepts that he followed to the letter, and then others he couldn't see the point of. For example, being wary of anyone who was not a Hasid.

He sometimes thought that he was unlucky to have been born into a religion that didn't suit him. Or else, that he was the misfit and other people were right not to respect him. In New York, it seemed to him, religion was not as much of a burden. "I was happy, my mother was still alive, everything was simple and straightforward."

On Shabbat, he went to eat at the home of the uncle and aunt who had raised him, but who had not managed to pass on all their values to him. As Hershey grew older, he felt bad for them. He would have really liked to make them happy. But he could never have made them happy unless he had been born a different person, or unless his mother had not died. Pleasing them meant getting married, but since his wife had died, it meant getting married again, having children, being devout like a real Hasid, staying inside the synagogue until prayers were over without slipping out to smoke a cigarette on the street corner. Pleasing them meant making money, commanding the respect of the community, and, above all, not associating with godless people. That was a lot. It was much too much for someone with his capacity for obedience. To obey without knowing the reason why — that was not for Hershey Rozenfeld. He felt he was already doing a lot to be accepted. It was just as easy to take their sarcasm, to which he had become accustomed, and take refuge in his own world while waiting for better days to come.

Better days would indeed come, and the bird with the broken wing would be embraced by his adoptive family and become a respectable man in the eyes of the community.

Since the age of fourteen – he was now thirty-eight – he had been working here and there, at all kinds of jobs. He had been employed by the neighbourhood Hasids and often by the Goys. Not that he became rich or anything, but he earned enough to pay his uncle room and board and then enough to get married. After his marriage ended so abruptly, he was happy to stay on alone in his little Hutchison Street apartment, a neat and tidy half-basement apartment that he was quite fond of.

He had been working at St-Viateur Bagel for three years. Of all the jobs he had ever had, this was the one he liked the most, by far. He loved the atmosphere of the bakery. All kinds of people came in and out, sniffing with delight at their bags of bagels. He, too, loved to breathe in the aroma of the bakery, and to feel the satiny flour on his fingers and the soft dough on his hands. It reminded him of when he was little and his mother would give him a piece of dough to play with, as she worked wonders with the pastry and told stories in her melodious voice. He would cut the dough up into long strips, knead them lovingly, and then shape them into smaller pieces that he twisted into well-formed circles. After tossing them in boiling water, he would coat the bagels with a crunchy topping of sesame or poppy seeds and cook them to perfection in a wood-fired oven.

One of his pals, someone he had worked with since starting at the bakery, came into some money one day. His friend inherited a tidy sum, which he wanted to put to good use without fretting about it too much. He just wanted to do something that would allow him to stop working. Without giving it a second thought, Hershey Rozenfeld said, "Let's open a bakery. I'll do the work, and you'll pocket the profits. I'll look after everything."

The idea of opening a bakery where they could make all kinds of bread and pastries was a real shot in the arm for Hershey, unleashing a newfound resourcefulness. He honestly didn't know he had it in him. He often thought about his mother, and he felt good, he felt he was on the right track. In less than two days, he found a storefront to rent on Bernard Street, just big enough, not too expensive. It was perfect. Hashem was omniscient, omnipresent, smiling down on him, and Hershey loved his God, too.

From then on, everything was smooth sailing.

It had to be a kosher bakery. The neighbourhood was overflowing with Hasidic families and he wanted their business. But he also wanted the others, the ones his aunt called the non-believers. The bakery had to be a pleasant place that would attract them, those people, but Hershey was not sure how to go about it.

His friend, Mr. Moneybags, had the clever idea of hiring a designer, someone who had turned a dark, dilapidated space on Saint-Laurent Boulevard into a scintillating boutique where passersby, himself included, would step in just to take a peek at the decor and then end up buying something. Hershey barely knew what the word "designer" meant, but he trusted his friend, and telephoned the designer, who turned out to be Lebanese. Everyone says that the Arabs and Jews don't get along, but it is not necessarily so. In this case, the Jew and the Lebanese got on like a house on fire.

The bakery was so beautiful that it caught the eye of all the passersby. A celestial light shining through a domed skylight attracted customers and had a soothing effect on them once they were inside. Everything looked good, and everything tasted good. It was the only kosher store in the neighbourhood where Jews and non-Jews congregated comfortably. The bakery was always full of satisfied customers, who could grab a coffee while waiting their turn. Friday afternoons were hectic, as families prepared for Shabbat. According to custom, Hershey closed the store before sundown on Friday and reopened on Sunday morning.

It was just like a Hasidic or Arabic folk tale. All of the people who had made fun of Hershey, who had ridiculed him and ostracized him, came in one after the other to buy his bread and his cakes, all the while bowing and scraping and addressing him as Mister Rozenfeld, if you please.

He had not become the most devout nor the best person, but in the eyes of his people, he had become richer and thus more respectable. As people used to say in the olden days, and it still holds true today:

Magically,
Money
Slips a silken shawl
Onto the beggar's shoulders
Erasing the traces
Of his failings and flaws.

THE DIARY OF HINDA ROCHEL

I said to Mama, "All the neighbours plant flowers in front of their houses. We never do." My mother looked at me strangely. She said, "We do things that they don't do. And they do things that we don't do. That's the way it is and it's not going to change." I asked her, "Is it part of our religion not to plant flowers? Does God like flowers?" She replied, "I don't know whether God likes flowers or not, but I don't have time for that kind of thing. Have you ever seen me sitting around with nothing to do?" "No, you are always working." "There, that's your answer. Watch out! Moishy is going to fall. I asked you to look after your brother."

My mother was busy washing the kitchen walls. The walls have always looked clean to me, but not to her. I have never seen her sitting down in an armchair. Even when we are eating, she gets up from the table twenty times. She likes to work more than anything else in the world, that's what I think. On Shabbat she HAS to rest. But it's very hard for her to rest.

"Go fill up the big pot with fresh water."

Commanders in the Israeli army must have the same kind of voice as my mother, even though they speak Hebrew and not Yiddish. You can never say no. You just obey. I'm tired of obeying. There's always someone I have to look after, always something I have to dust, wash, peel, stir, iron. I never get a break. Thank goodness there's school. Yehuda does nothing. Nothing. His royal highness has become a *bocher*. He's thirteen. That gives him all kinds of rights and privileges. Since his bar mitzvah, it's gotten worse. He even acts like a king. He's one year older than I am. It's not fair. What's more, there are only boys in my family. I'm really unlucky.

ANTONELLA ROSSETTI

Every year she felt the same impatience, the same joy and the same anticipation. On the days when the bags of topsoil were delivered, the weather was always nice on Hutchison. Without fail. She was delighted, of course. She took full advantage of every fine day, more than anyone else. During the warm weather, she relived her childhood, spent in a small village in southern Italy where she had walked around barefoot, carefree and happy. Her little postage-stamp garden to the left of her front staircase was the same. It was her own little Italy. It was her very own. Even when her husband was still alive, she, Antonella Rossetti, was the one who looked after the front garden. Marco was in charge of the vegetable garden in the backyard. She had since taken that one over too, but her undying pleasure lay in cultivating the one out front.

It wasn't just the way the earth felt on her hands and feet, and knees as well, not just the tomatoes that she pampered continually in good weather and bad, not just the basil that she grew amongst the few flowers she planted — a new variety every year. What she liked most of all were the looks she got from people as they walked past her house.

91

She had a full head of hair, which shone as if she had coloured it the day before, and she was always artfully coiffed with superb French twists or elaborate chignons. Antonella was beautiful, stylish and proud of the good looks she still had in her seventies. She specially liked the slightly envious way people stared at her. What a beautiful garden, the smiling passersby seemed to be thinking, what beautiful tomatoes you have there! They would slow down and take a good look, and once a woman even stopped and asked her outright if she could taste one of them. "Not ready yet," Antonella replied. "Two days. You come back, two days." The woman had indeed come back, and to Antonella's amusement, she had held the sun-soaked red tomato in her hands; she stroked it, sniffed it, and then bit into it with her eyes shut tight. It reminded Antonella of taking holy communion, and perhaps that's what the woman was thinking too.

With money handy to pay for the delivery of the top-soil, Antonella waited, visibly impatient, for the driver to leave. In the cardboard box on her balcony, her rakes, shovels and buckets were already waiting as anxiously as she was to touch the earth after such a long winter. For Antonella, each year brought the same sense of wonder. As if the long winters almost made her forget that spring would come on time, and that she could once again grow the most beautiful tomatoes on Hutchison Street. "Would you like me to spread it?" the driver asked. She understood the meaning of the sentence, but not the word "spread." It was the first time that a delivery man had offered to help her. Did she look that old, *madre mia*? As ever, she didn't want anyone else touching her garden. "No, no, *grazie*. I like very much ..." She made the motion of spreading earth. The driver understood that it was time to ask her to sign the papers, take her money and leave.

Her garden was at a higher level than all the other gardens on the street and, from year to year, picking up earth made it overflow onto the sidewalk. Last year she even had to build a kind of box with high sides to keep the dirt from spilling outside of the wrought iron fence. A handwritten sign hung on her fence in winter and summer, on which she had written, in misspelled French, "*Pas bicicle icite*."

There were several Italian families living on Hutchison when Antonella first moved in with her husband and children forty years ago. Back then, people tried to keep up with one another as far as gardens were concerned, and tomatoes and grapevines were a favourite. They constructed vine-covered arbours, and would try to coax the vines into producing not only tender leaves that could be stuffed – the envy of the Lebanese – but also black, red or green grapes, which were delicious to eat and so mouthwatering that they made the other neighbours jealous. Between Bernard and Saint-Viateur, there was only one arbour left, worthy of the name, which belonged to Antonella's second neighbours, the Marconis. Gradually the families had become better off. They had moved to Laval or elsewhere, and the vines had dried up from lack of care or know-how. The Jewish mothers had too many children and not enough time to look after vines, let alone gardens.

When Antonella was not busy digging, hoeing, prop-
agating, thinning out, pruning and weeding, or just ad-
miring her own garden, she like to get all spruced up.
She would spray herself with perfume, put on her high-
heeled shoes – not too high, though – and then go out for
a walk around the neighbourhood. She would take the
time to go shopping and sit on a bench on the street or in
the park in the summertime. In preparation for Sunday
dinner with her children, she would shop at Four Brothers and then have her order delivered, picking up a few
other items that she bought at Latina. Sunday night dinner took place every week without fail even if one or two
of her children were missing. Too bad for the ones who
didn't come because Antonella's meals were delicious, and
good for the ones who showed up, because there would
be even more left over for them to take home.

Ever since she retired, her meals had become feasts. She
put in all the time and attention that was needed, and she
watched cooking shows religiously. Even if she didn't understand everything people were saying, she got ideas just
from watching. She really liked the little di Stasio woman,
perhaps because she was of Italian background, and Antonella was very touched the time she went on a trip to
Italy. Her Italian accent left something to be desired, but
still, it was better than nothing, and Antonella liked her
anyway because she was cheerful and loved food. In the
afternoon, she watched *Pour le plaisir* on French television,
because she found both the hosts funny and always in a
good mood. She also watched Italian programs when she

could pick them up on cable.

Antonella Rossetti definitely had a knack for looking on the bright side of things all of the time. She had understood once and for all that it's not worth taking things the wrong way, or going against the tide. Naturally, she had been a bit down when her husband died, just as they were about to retire. They could have had a few more good years together. She loved her Marco so much, but crying wouldn't bring him back. Of course, when she arrived in Canada at the age of sixteen without her family, she had felt homesick. She had been nostalgic for her childhood, she was lonesome for her parents, and she missed the year-round hot weather, the feel of the ground under her bare feet, and the scent of the orange trees. But she liked the work that they found for her as a seamstress in a factory on Castelnau Street. The noise was irritating, but you got used to it. She had girlfriends who were fun to be with, and they all worked hard and laughed a lot.

Antonella liked to laugh. To get dolled up, do her hair and step out. She liked it when people looked at her and suggested, with a little smile, that she was not bad for an old girl! She loved the smell of earth and the feel of her hands in the earth. She loved her children. She loved them even when they didn't come for dinner, when they found excuses not to come at the last minute, even after she had cooked up a lot of good food, especially for them, making it exactly the way they liked it. Antonella was just like that, she had a gift for taking life as it comes, and never looking back.

THE DIARY OF HINDA ROCHEL

I would like to be someone else. Not me, Hinda Rochel, the daughter of Sholem and Chevda. It's not that I don't love my father and mother and my brothers. It's just that I am tired of my life. Sometimes I'm . . . I don't know how to say this. Pure, impure, it's as if there were only two words in my mother's language. Rules to follow and things to do. That's it. Pure, impure, permitted, forbidden. Many more things are forbidden than permitted. Like the French language. There are way too many grammar rules in French. It's the same thing in our religion. It's so hard. In French, there are exceptions to the rules, but not in our religion. There are no exceptions. Everything is by the book. I can never tell anyone what I'm writing about in my journal, not even my best friend. That's what my life is like. I'm looking forward to having my own home, with no one to tell me what to do. To having a bit of peace. When I'm at home, I often feel like crying. But where can I cry without having someone scold me for crying? I don't even have my own room. Two of my little brothers sleep in my room. In the winter, it's even worse. The bathroom? I have never been able to lock myself in the bathroom for more than three minutes at a time. When I feel like crying there's always someone who has to do something you can't write about in a diary. May the Creator forgive me, I hate life, and I hate MY life even MORE.

SYLVAIN TREMBLAY

He had always hated seeing his mother with her eyes brimming with tears. Tears that never flowed. She must have been about fifty-five or fifty-six years old when he noticed it, suddenly, and it began to get on his nerves, and then to horrify him. Every time she told a little story about the past, no matter whether it was happy or unhappy, her eyes would mist over, covered in a layer of tears that she never shed. He wanted to tell her: have a good cry so we can get it over with. But even before he could blurt out the words, his mother's tears would disappear. And then appear again when she got the least bit emotional. It would only take some innocuous anecdote, sad, happy or full of tenderness. You never knew when hidden feelings would well up and when her heart would spill over into her eyes.

The frequency of these episodes drove him crazy. Where had she been hiding her pain for all those years? She had seemed so happy.

Around the same age, Sylvain Tremblay began to experience the same terrible affliction as his mother. He had just turned fifty-five. To his great dismay, he could not keep his feelings from bubbling up to his eyes, making his eyelids and entire face puffy, and filling his eyes with fluid that couldn't find the exit valve. He had picked up his mother's revolting condition. His fits of emotion were unpredictable, he would become agitated more and more often, but tears never flowed from his eyes.

Many years ago, Sylvain Tremblay was a popular singer. He couldn't walk down the street without being recognized by someone. People would sometimes come up to him and talk. Some would ask him for his autograph, while others pretended not to recognize him, although it showed anyway. He liked his profession, but he didn't really like to be recognized. It even irritated him sometimes. Being well known goes hand in hand with being recognized, and he had no idea that one day he would miss both.

His career had begun with a bang, without any particular effort on his part, and he coasted on his success. Shows, television, going on the road — it worked well for some years, until he felt the urge to compose his own songs. One or two of them were played on the radio. He was thrilled to hear his fans singing his very own words, to a tune he had composed. But it was short-lived. You can't change styles without impunity, people in the entertainment business would say. The pop singer had lost sight of his niche, and the composer-songwriter was not able to carve out one of his own. His audiences, those greedy, nameless people, as fickle as the wind, had not stuck by him. "My dear audience," Marc Labrèche so affectionately repeated every week, to butter up his spectators and win their loyalty, because, to be honest, a performer is nobody without his audience. In Sylvain Tremblay's case, the people who had fallen in love with him on a whim forgot him just as quickly, without so much as a goodbye.

The more time went by the less hope he held out.

Revival, resurrection. He had tried many times, of course. He had written a bunch of new songs. But these efforts never paid off. There was no reaction from audiences or from the entertainment world. Too many excellent young songwriters were popping up – young women and men who had something to say and a new way of making music. There were too many good songs on the air. He felt old, obsolete and decrepit. Frustrated and defeated, he buried his self-confidence ten feet underground.

And time passed. No one recognized him anymore, no one talked about him. There wasn't the slightest reference to him on the radio, even in jest. Nothing. He was working as a car salesman and earning a good living at it, incognito. None of the people he worked with knew he had once had his moment of glory, that he had been on television so many times, or that he had performed in the biggest concert halls in Montreal and beyond. He didn't ever talk about it. Why would he? There was no point in making himself feel more ashamed.

And still, when he was not dragged down by his urge to sing again, Sylvain Tremblay wasn't what you would call a happy man – that would be a stretch – but he wasn't unhappy either, even though sporadic surges of ambition were constantly ruining his life. He wanted to plan a comeback. "But what am I going to revive?" he asked himself one day. "What am I going to revive?" It triggered such strong emotion that tears began to flow. He thought of his mother, and sobbed until he was exhausted.

One day, as he was still grappling with the decision to give up his now-defunct past, another nail was hammered into its coffin. He received a mysterious phone call from a woman he didn't know. She was a researcher for a television show on "has-beens," looking for old stars who were willing to talk about what they were now up to.

It could not have been more humiliating for him. As he talked to the researcher, he remembered a saying he had read somewhere, about an old hero who does not want to talk about his glorious past. She bombarded him with references to his past as a pop singer. He blushed and his eyes brimmed with tears. He wanted to tell her about his recent songs, which were ready to be recorded, if only he could find a record company.

It was humiliating, but he couldn't refuse. You never know, this was perhaps a way to kick start his career again. A producer might be watching, or a far-sighted manager, or a record company. You never know.

When he saw the television guys arrive at his place, he shuddered with fear but still felt vaguely happy. It was now or never. He had to go ahead with it. With all his heart.

In the blink of an eye, a crew armed with cameras, cables, spotlights, lapel-mics, make-up – the whole kit and caboodle – set up their gear in the nicest room in his apartment, his living room which overlooked Hutchison. He had cleaned house, tidied up, rearranged the living room to make it look spiffy, but on orders from the producer, they turned everything topsy-turvy in the space of a few minutes. Witnessing this commotion made Sylvain relive the excitement of his early years. Tears welled up in his eyes. Too many emotions at once, a mix of old and new ones. He had more stage fright than he'd ever had. He had to get through it at all costs. He took refuge in his bathroom, where he tried to relax and perk himself up by splashing cold water on his face.

It was like a dream, or rather a nightmare. He could hear the hubbub. They were calling him, they were saying his name. It had been a long time since he had heard the sound of his own name. His confidence came back. He quickly dried his face off, pasted a smile on it and made his way into the living room. It was now or never.

A few weeks later, Sylvain Tremblay was sitting in front of the television in his chaotic living room, which the camera crew had left in disarray. "Sorry, Monsieur Tremblay, we're in a bit of a rush, you don't mind, do you?" No, he had just wanted them to bugger off as soon as possible!

When he saw himself, he was ashamed. A total loser. Pitiful. What's more, what they were talking about was out of date, songs that didn't mean anything anymore, even to him. They were playing excerpts they had dredged up from god knows where. So ridiculous. Enough to

make you cry your eyes out. Not only was he ashamed
to see how absolutely useless he was, but he also noticed
that he'd become the spitting image of his mother. He
had the same way of holding back the tears. It was scary.
He had always been told that he looked like his father.
What had happened to him in such a short time? And his
nose, what had happened to his nose? He was overcome
with emotion and his face was ablaze and contorted. It
was pathetic. How he had aged! Wrinkles everywhere.
And his smile, which everyone had complimented him on
when he was young, was stiff and austere now. Luckily,
he hadn't shed any tears. Christ, that would have been the
last straw, ludicrous beyond belief, the height of the absurd: an old singer crying over his past. There is nothing
more lame than that. A tear on his swollen and blotchy
nose … minus the wit and panache of a Cyrano.

He turns the television off before the end of the credits.
He has a bit of a stomach ache and feels like he's going to
puke. He takes a deep breath, as he used to do before going out on stage. He breathes in and out a few times while
looking out the window. He calms down. He will never
sing in public anymore. It's over. He will plunk away on
his guitar by himself, in his living room, to hear his own
voice, his own words. He'll sing for friends if they ask
him to, but nothing more.

Outside, two Hasidim are walking by. Each one has a
cell phone glued to his ear. At least they have not seen the
show. An older couple walks by, arm in arm. You can't

tell which one is propping the other up, but it's all right, they're getting around without too much trouble. Two young people are standing in the middle of the sidewalk with their arms around each other. They can't stop kissing. He is moved as he watches them. He thinks of a song that he could write, exactly from this perspective.

While his faded image was being displayed on one channel, a million other images were flooding the one hundred and eighty other channels. At that very moment, children were being born and others were dying of hunger and thirst, while he, Sylvain Tremblay, was fretting over a lousy thirty-minute show that had been plugged into the schedule of TVA.

No.

All of a sudden, he turns around and looks straight ahead into the room. He decides to tidy up his apartment. Neither sad nor joyful, he puts the pieces of furniture back in place. He feels almost light, as if an enormous weight has just slipped off his shoulders. Maybe that's what they mean when they say that you have to reach rock bottom before you can find your way back up. His past has been put to rest once and for all thanks to this grotesque half-hour of television which has placed a tombstone over his years of waiting and hoping for nothing. It's over. There's no looking back. His future will be whatever he makes of it.

The telephone rings. His first reflex is not to answer. What if a workmate has recognized him? He doesn't feel up to talking about it. Then he changes his mind.

"Yes, this is Sylvain Tremblay, yes … Thank you,

that's nice ... Yes, yes, I know who you are, I often listen to your songs on the radio ... I'm still writing, yes ... You want to hear them? Why? ... No, I've never thought about it, but why not? ... I've done a hundred or so ... You want to come around? ... Yes, a home recording, of course. I'll sing you the other ones and play my guitar ... I'm here, you can come right over. I live in Mile End."

He gives the person his address, hangs up and continues to rearrange things in his living room. "How stupid can I be! All these years, I've been an idiot, fighting this useless battle. I've had a one-track mind, that's what. I've had blinders on. I've never looked left or right, I've just spent my time banging my head against a brick wall. I've been obsessive, to say the least. It never even occurred to me. It's incredible. Dear God, let other people sing my friggin' tunes. "A lyricist is a writer who sings," as the French songwriter Pierre Delanoë used to say. He was right. And I know how to compose music as well. Terrific! I will finally hear my songs. If they're sung by other people, so be it. I will finally hear them. Yes, yes, yes!

He was still laughing when the doorbell rang.

THE ACTRESSES

A few doors down from Bernard, on the Mile End side of the street, there was a second-floor apartment in a building with a spiral staircase. They called it the actresses' apartment. One actress would arrive, live there for a few years, and then disappear. Another one would move in, live there for a time, and then vanish in turn, leaving room for the next one. There were never any male actors or ordinary people. Always actresses.

There was never a sign saying "apartment for rent." And yet, the apartment never stayed empty. You would think the place belonged to the Artists Union and that it was awarded through a competition process, but open to female actors only because it would have been surprising that no male actor had won the competition in forty years. A lot of actors came around as friends or lovers, or with a script in hand to rehearse, but none of them came as tenants.

Some of the actresses were well known thanks to television, while others worked in the theatre and were not known to the general public. When you saw how discreet and self-effacing they looked doing their shopping on Park Avenue, working out at the YMCA, or running in their jogging pants year-round, you wouldn't have believed they were able to face large audiences in the theatres of Montreal, where they had nonetheless played important roles at one time or another. All of the women who had lived in the apartment, one after the other, had enjoyed successful careers on the stage, on television or in the movies. Some of them continued to act, while others had given up the business, or rather the business had given up on them. The ones who had lived here in the 1970s or 1980s were now fifty or sixty years old, or more … "There are not a lot of parts for people our age, the most difficult thing in our business is to survive." That's what they all say, pretty much in those words, when they have the opportunity to speak in public.

In the neighbourhood, they go unnoticed. None of them was a big star, but they were all accomplished artists, well regarded by their peers. None of them signed autographs, not even the day after a big opening at a company such as the Théâtre du Nouveau Monde. In this diverse neighbourhood, there are few francophones, and even fewer theatre-goers.

None of the actresses fit the exuberant image usually associated with performers. Except when one of them ran into someone from her own circle on the street. It would take no longer than one second for all traces of the unassuming and discreet persona to vanish. It was an instant transformation. The woman with her head down in the grocery store or some other place would become an actress in all her glory, playing her seduction scene from act one, two or three, at the corner of Bernard and Hutchison. Her voice would ring out, her eyes would shine, and she would make sweeping gestures. It would depend, of course, on the person she was facing and on what she had to gain from using her charm in this improvised form of theatre. Perhaps it wasn't to "gain" anything at all. Instead, it might have been the sheer pleasure of running into a friend, of being recognized by someone, of being totally herself and rediscovering the multiple personality traits that can only be deployed among people of like mind.

A few days ago, a new tenant moved into the actresses' apartment. She is the complete opposite of her colleagues, in that she is constantly performing. As soon as she walks down the stairs, she looks around to see who is watching her. She pretends she is on the red carpet, she hears the paparazzi snapping pictures of her and she pictures a crowd of admirers waiting for her to sign her photograph.

Younger than all the others who have preceded her, she is flamboyant, made up, with her hair deliberately tousled, carefully and stylishly dressed ... just to go to the corner store.

As if there were a camera to the right of the cash register, she strikes an affected pose, but the cashier is in a hurry and serves her without a glance. She wiggles her pretty derrière as she strolls along and goes back up to the apartment building. Before going inside, she turns around as if to go down the stairs again, she leans on the balcony railing, scans the street, and then shrugs her shoulders with a defeated look. No one has noticed her. She spins around and goes in.

She is not expected to last long in this motley neighbourhood, which is sure to dampen her spirits. Considering that seventy-five per cent of the people are Hasidim, who don't look at anyone, it would come as no surprise if depression got the best of the young actress sooner or later.

MADELEINE DESROCHERS

Madeleine Desrochers was definitely a happy person. Since she was a teenager, she had known where she was going and what would make her happy: looking after people in need.

She took pleasure in giving. The more she gave, the more she had to give. She thrived on giving to others and giving of herself. She didn't need anything else to be happy, and she didn't expect compliments or gratitude. Of course, she liked it when people said thank you, but she didn't expect more than that. When her work paid off, she was delighted, but she was not discouraged by failure either. Quite the contrary. It meant that there was still a lot to do, and she was determined to do as much as she possibly could.

Right up until the day when she fell to the ground like a ton of bricks, unable to get up again on her own.

Amateur psychologists, and even real ones, would have said that Madeleine Desrochers didn't know her limits, that she had gone too far, and that by looking after others she had neglected herself.

She, on the other hand, was convinced that the way

she lived her life was perfectly consistent with her nature, that her energy was renewable, that her strength could be renewed by a good night's sleep, and that even if she was satisfied with what she had already accomplished, she could always do better.

There was so much to do!

She worked as a nurse, she volunteered to help young alcoholics and drug addicts, and she launched a foundation that provided aid for children in Togo and Benin. That was her life. Her whole life.

Madeleine Desrochers was like some artists. She did not lose herself in her work. Instead, work was a form of self-expression.

What more can you ask of life if you are happy? What more can you ask for when you are fulfilling your dreams every day and accomplishing what you have set out to do?

When disaster struck, she lost her flexibility and strength all at once. She had bent down to pick up a small battery-operated radio that a patient had accidentally dropped. She had one knee on the floor, with one arm stretched out under the bed to pick it up. She began to tremble and her right knee swelled up before her very eyes. She then felt what seemed like an electric shock in her back and hips and she was overcome by indescribable pain. It was Madame Therrien, the patient, who rang for help again and again, while Madeleine tried to get up, to no avail.

When she was born, she was blessed with constant energy and an unusually strong mental and physical constitution. She was cheerful and always looked on the bright side of things. She got by with only six hours of sleep, after which she was once again in gear. If you had seen her striding down the hallways of the Hôtel-Dieu hospital, you would never have believed she was already fifty-two years old.

Believe it or not, even though she had always spent time with sick people and sickness, Madeleine Desrochers didn't know what it was like to be sick herself. Not really. A few colds, a flu once in a while, that was the sum total of her personal maladies. She had never dreamt that one day, she, too, would perhaps ...

When she was a child, she had seen her mother suffer, often in bed, while her father was the picture of health, until the day he dropped dead suddenly. Madeleine had inherited her father's genes. Her mother had said to her one day, "I don't wish it upon you, my dear, God knows I don't wish it upon you, but you won't really understand until your own body is affected." She often thought about her mother now that her body had given up on her.

Irony number one: This was the first time that she had been a guinea pig in the convoluted maze of the health-care system. With her nightgown open at the back, and her bum exposed, lying on a stretcher pushed about by strangers, high-spirited Madeleine was in too much pain to be in good spirits, so much so that she wanted to cry instead.

Irony number two: She was surrounded by doctors, specialists of all sorts, and she knew them all well. They were competent all right, but no one could tell her exactly what was wrong with her. She took a battery of tests, of course, and was scrutinized by the most sophisticated machinery. Each doctor sent her on to the next, until they ran out of colleagues to send her to. They didn't agree with one another. The words *rheumatoid* and *acute attack* were repeated the most often. But she was convinced that she had picked up a lousy infection or virus that had not yet been identified, a nasty bug that was causing her a lot of pain. *Tabarouette*, as her father used to say, to avoid actually swearing. A royal pain in the arse. Although they didn't have a precise diagnosis, they did give her anti-inflammatories and powerful pain-killers. There was a shortage of beds, so they politely released her from hospital, plunked her in a taxi, and told her to get plenty of rest, as if she was capable of doing anything else.

Irony number three: Had it not been for the young person from Togo who had been living with her for a year, Madeleine Desrochers, who had helped so many people all her life, would have been up shit creek without a paddle, as people used to say back in her home town.

Madeleine had been living on her own since she had lost the love of her life at the age of thirty-nine. Since then, she had had a fling or two, but nothing out of this world, nothing good enough to replace her first love, in any case. And then, there was no one in her life anymore. She had a lot of women friends. But friendships, like patients, need to be looked after, as she well knew. Her friends were not needy, and they had other friends, but the young druggies and the children in Togo and Benin only had her.

Gradually, the telephone stopped ringing. And it was not because Madeleine now had time on her hands, lots of time, because she could no longer walk down the four steps of her staircase, that her friends would start coming around again, as if by magic.

She didn't hold it against them and she had no regrets. It was her life. The life she had chosen.

She was forced to retire and, since then, her body and her mind had become an occupied territory, taken over by illness. She would be crushed by acute pain, when she wasn't feeling totally comatose. She had a lot of trouble moving around and a sharp pain would shoot down her body even when she was lying down. Her aches and pains were nearly unbearable and drained the little energy she had left. Intense fatigue – that strange thing she had known only by name – had insidiously conquered her entire body and even altered her mind.

She had the feeling that her *real* life was already behind her. In the years she had left, a reprieve, she would lead a life that was foreign to her, but she had to get used to it, for lack of anything better.

The question that she didn't dare ask was, "Am I going to be like this for the rest of my days?"

After the death of her beloved Jacques, Madeleine had shared her Hutchison Street apartment with her friend Irene, who was also a nurse. Not long after, Irene left to go live and work in Togo with her new husband, who was a male nurse originally from there. Since then, Madeleine had been taking in students as boarders. There was a bedroom and sitting room separated by a sliding door, also known as a double living room. It was very cheap and rarely stayed empty. Her apartment was long and narrow, as is often the case on Hutchison, which made it easy for young tenants to feel at home and invite friends in. There was a common washroom and tenants had access to the kitchen, where they could even invite a gang over for supper. On condition that they let Madeleine know in advance. She almost always agreed. She liked young people. And they liked her. They would include her, she would have a drink with them, have a bite, and then leave them alone while she slipped into her room where she had her books and a second television set. The large kitchen would come to life again, just like the days when Jacques was still alive and they entertained a lot. She would listen to them talking and laughing and she couldn't have been happier had they been her own children. The next morning, when she went into the kitchen to have breakfast at her table beside the window, everything would be spic and span, the dishes washed, the beer and wine bottles disposed of in the recycling bin. The students were always the ones who took the recycling and garbage bags out. The rules of the house were clear and everything was tickety-boo. Madeleine wondered why adults complained about young people. The ones who had lived with her had always kept their word.

Nzimbou was the latest one. Her friends called her Zim or Zimou. She not only kept her word, like the young people who had lived there before, but she was extraordinarily gentle and caring. You have no idea how much the slightest kindness, which would have meant nothing to someone in good health, helped to comfort Madeleine, who was helpless, practically disabled. Irene had written to her from Togo, and had recommended this beautiful woman Nzimbou. She was quite simply a godsend, an angel.

And it was this angel who introduced Madeleine Desrochers to the internet, which changed the disabled woman into a world traveller.

Nzimbou had come to Quebec to study computer science, a field that fascinated her more and more. As with all passionate people, Nzimbou's enthusiasm knew no bounds. She had been talking to Madeleine about the internet for a long time. She had vaunted its advantages and multiple uses, telling her about social networks that could be set up and accessed from home. It was not that Madeleine lacked intelligence, but she found the world of computers intangible and hence incomprehensible. By comparison, fairy tales in which carriages turn into pumpkins, even the story of Aladdin and his magic lamp, seemed more plausible. At work, she had learned to enter information into a computer, that was the extent of it, and now this young Togolese was telling her that she could communicate with the entire world. For her, "it just didn't compute," as the Americans would say, until Nzimbou began talking to her about philanthropy and pointed out that the foundation she had set up to help children in Togo and Benin would be able to use the internet for fundraising.

Philanthropy, a magic word, suddenly lifted her spirits, and Madeleine was all ears. But Nzimbou, who was a smart cookie, understood that no matter how much she talked and explained, no matter how willing Madeleine was to listen, it was not enough. She also had to see the miracle with her own eyes.

She needed to get hooked up to the internet right away. High speed, wireless, while we're at it, and why not a high-performance laptop computer? With her landlady's credit card in hand, Nzimbou made all the arrangements while Madeleine lay on her couch doing nothing, pumped full of pain killers, patiently awaiting the miracle.

Nzimbou enjoyed playing the role of magician, if only to see Madeleine's mounting delight and amazement. Nzimbou was a good teacher – that was what she wanted to do with her life – and Madeleine was a good pupil, who was rediscovering the joy of learning. She remembered being in grade one, when a few letters magically became a word or two, and then a sentence. Now, as before, she saw a world open before her, wider and wider each step of the way. How had she managed to live until now without being part of it, without even having an inkling of its existence? Everything was at her fingertips. She could see and hear what she wanted, she could discover new things, study, look things up in encyclopedias, consult specialists, sign petitions, take part in discussion forums, and even laugh. It would take more than a single lifetime to see everything that was available. The only things missing in this great adventure were smelling and touching, but Madeleine felt that she had used both of these senses too much in her previous life.

Nzimbou was delighted to finally have access to her Hotmail account without going to a coffee shop or the university. She could do her homework and send the assignments in by email while Madeleine was resting. The creation of an attractive and efficient website for the Foundation was coming along. She had spoken to her professor who was very open to the idea, and he even agreed to give her credit for her work on the project.

The training sessions took place either at the kitchen table when Madeleine's back and legs allowed her to sit up, or at the comfortable sofa in the sitting room next to the kitchen. One day, there was a moment of magic. Madeleine had said, "If you can see the whole world, show me your country." Does Togo exist on the internet? Nzimbou had never thought of checking. Suddenly, she was afraid that she wouldn't find Togo, such a small country to which everyone but Madeleine and a few people like her were oblivious. Two or three clicks later, the map of the huge African continent came up. Then she zoomed in on West Africa, and Togo appeared. She got goose bumps all over. In less than a second, she found Lomé, where she was born and where her whole family still lived. Everything was still there, just as it was before she left.

Nzimbou was much more moved than she let on. Madeleine, too. This little journey, albeit a virtual one, had made her understand something about the young woman, about her origins – she didn't know exactly what. She looked at Nzimbou and, at that very second, it was as if she were seeing her for the first time. A current of affection and recognition ran between them. A sisterly bond had been kindled despite all the borders that separated them.

It's crazy how a single image can arouse and expose feelings that are sometimes difficult to put into words. But between you and me, do you really have to say everything?

FRANÇOISE CAMIRAND

She saw her coming from a distance. She stood out because of her long grey hair, her faded clothing and her tottering gait.

Jacinthe Beaulieu is crossing the street without even looking to see whether any cars are coming, and then she passes Françoise without seeing her. Her complexion is pasty like that of the Hasidic men.

Listening to her babbling incomprehensibly, Françoise immediately thinks of Jacinthe's children, who are now big. They have been marked forever, even if their mother no longer has relapses, because you can never completely recover from your childhood.

Very quickly, Françoise goes up to her office. She feels the weight of all the suffering in the world, and she hasn't had the time to protect herself. In front of her computer screen, she wipes away the tears and begins to work.

She had often seen Jacinthe Beaulieu, sitting alone in front of a cup of coffee smoking cigarette after cigarette in the days when you could still smoke in a restaurant. Sometimes, too, in Outremont Park with her son and daughter, old before their time, with an unimaginable sadness in their eyes. They would sit close to their mother. They didn't play like the other children. She spoke to them in a gentle voice, she told them to go play, but they didn't move. One day, she went to sit on a swing. They followed her, and got on the swings beside her, which were free.

"Do you want me to give you a push, sweetheart?"

Françoise remembered the words, the sweet sound of her voice. Seeing what a state Jacinthe was in, she knew that she couldn't give a push to anyone at that time. She was the one who really needed one ... Her demons had taken over.

Jacinthe Beaulieu, whom her parents called Cynthia with undying love ...

Life is cruel. There's so much love proffered with nothing in return. It's beyond belief. How can we come to terms with life?

Even though she knew that Jacinthe's life was a hellish roller coaster, she wanted to write about it with a smile, to find a glimmer of hope in it. In thirty years of writing, she had learned that you sometimes have to stand back a bit in order to grasp your subject better. Like the painter, who steps back, squints, and stands at a distance from his model in order to see her better.

JACINTHE BEAULIEU

She often wished she had never been born.

Jacinthe Beaulieu's existence teetered between going through hell and being afraid of it. If a patch of blue appeared in the sky, it soon got covered over by clouds of apprehension. You might as well do without the sunshine.

At times she would thank God for the flashes of light He gave her, and at other times, she was damned mad at Him for taking her wits away without thinking for a single second that she needed all her marbles to raise her children.

No one had been spared in this mental fiasco. Her eldest daughter could be blown over by the slightest gust of wind, and her son was a carbon copy of her. Although she asked, why her, why him, why me, God didn't answer. God, whom she continued to love despite everything, wasn't talking. You could say he was mute, actually. Genetics? She didn't understand it at all, although she tried to, she was its victim, that's all she knew. Fate? She wished she didn't know that word, which she found so absurd. Fate was a double-edged sword, as she well knew from experience, it depended on which head it was going to come down on. She was the one in her family, one out of the five children. The sharp edge of the knife had been pressed up against her throat, leaving her hanging on to life by just a thread.

Just enough to allow her to finish high school, before chaos set in. She didn't remember much about what had happened to her between the ages of sixteen and twenty. The baby growing in her belly brought her back to reality. She wanted to keep it. Her family had helped her and she gave birth to a healthy daughter, thank God. She had a year of relative calm during which her head let her live her life. Then she began going off the rails again. She heard voices once more, and she had to run away to escape them. After living out on the street, she landed in the hospital. But between the street and the hospital, another baby had popped up in her belly.

The medical treatment she got turned out to be miraculous. She began to believe in God, and in the medication she took assiduously, thanking God and her stock of pills for having saved her life.

Her head had given her a break for a while, but it was a precarious rest. Someone who has experienced that kind of meltdown is always on edge. Thanks to her meds and her parents, with whom she and the two kids lived, there was once again a glimmer of hope. Thanks to her strength of character, too. Jacinthe Beaulieu was brave. All she asked of God was to keep her from relapsing and to give her the strength to raise her children properly. She wanted to study, work, rent an apartment for herself and the kids, and become a self-sufficient and normal person.

One of her parents' neighbours taught her the techniques of Swedish massage. Jacinthe was good at it and the neighbour referred some of her clients to her. It was a new beginning. Jacinthe had her fingers crossed. She prayed to God, took her medication and found an apartment on Hutchison Street, not far from her parents' house. The apartment wasn't big, but it wasn't very expensive either. It was paradise! With support from social services to supplement her income, she had two whole years to look after her children, doing work that she loved. She enjoyed two years of stability, although she was always torn between latent anxiety and hope that was struggling to emerge. No one had declared a "cure" with a capital C and an exclamation point. But you never know, miracles are always possible, it has happened before. Lying on her bed, with her eyes closed, she would count the days since her last breakdown, and she would smile. She felt good, with her children asleep in the next room, and she told herself that all was well. Everything is going great. Maybe it will last. Maybe I'll have a nice life ...

She was taking her meds conscientiously, and her life appeared to be going well, when, without warning, disaster struck again and she was torn to shreds. That year, it knocked her off her feet with unprecedented intensity. Cynthia was devastated. Jacinthe was brought to her knees. She collapsed, and was out of it for several long months, during which she didn't even recognize her children.

It had been the same each time, for over twenty years.

As soon as Jacinthe's life began to have the semblance of a normal life, the beast struck her down again. Her children were caught up in a hit-and-miss cycle of breakdowns which they could feel coming on, hospitalizations and grandparents who did the best they could. Worrying about relapses, afraid of not recognizing their own mother anymore, and absolutely terrified that she would no longer recognize them, they ended up damaged by all the years of fear, helplessness and constant upset in their lives.

If you're ever on Hutchison and happen to meet a woman in her forties who looks like she has been to hell and back multiple times, if you hear her talking to herself or speaking to someone you can't see, don't be afraid. Treat her with kindness and smile at her, if you don't mind. In any case, she won't see you, because she's too busy struggling to avoid the troubles that are looming. If she's fucking pissed off at her stupid god-damned life, and can't find any other words to describe how she feels, it's because she's trying to offend her God, whom she loves dearly nonetheless, her God who's not very talkative and who's just let her down once again. When gods are like that, it's not really worth hanging on to them, is it? But Jacinthe Beaulieu, for one, believes it is.

THE DIARY OF HINDA ROCHEL

My cousin Srully is going to New York. My mother told me, and she is sad because she likes Srully a lot. She wanted him to become a rabbi. "In New York, he will never become a rabbi," my mother said.

I didn't tell her because she was feeling too bad, but I know that Srully doesn't want to be a rabbi. That's why he is going to leave. I remember that one day, when I was still little, Srully came to our house to borrow something from my father. While waiting for Papa to come home from work, Srully went to sit in the backyard and took out a book to study. I went up to him, and got very close to him. I would never do that today. I was little and I didn't know that you should not disturb someone who is studying. He asked me if I knew how to read and if I liked reading. I answered yes to both questions. Then he said, "Listen." He closed his book, closed his eyes, and recited a long passage by heart. It was very beautiful. Even though I understood almost nothing, I found it magnificent. It sounded like a song without a chorus. When he was finished, he opened his eyes and sat there for a long time without speaking. I was standing next to him. I kept very still even though when I was little I always squirmed a lot. Without looking at me, he asked,

"Do you like studying?" I said yes. "Would you like to study for your whole life?" I said yes. He looked at me as if he felt sorry for me. "You can't study, not even the Talmud, because you're a girl. That's why women must obey the laws without even understanding them. They don't have the right to study for a long time. I am lucky."

He kept quiet for a while. He closed his eyes. He said, "That's what I want to do. Spend my whole life studying. That's what I want."

All of that came back to me as soon as my mother told me Srully was leaving. I'll never forget Srully's voice when he said, "That's what I want to do, spend my whole life studying." Even though I was just a little girl back then, I will never forget. Never.

SRULLY

He was the fourth child in a family of ten children. The oldest were already married and had several children. He was next in line to get married. He hadn't been keen on the idea, not so far, even though his mother had already begun to hint that the sooner he got married the better, he was already nineteen years old.

But Srully loved to study. That's what he liked best in the whole world. He knew that it was honourable to support a family, and he knew that the community valued having as many children as possible. But he also knew that it was an enormous responsibility and that if he got married he would have less time to study.

He had thought of becoming a rabbi. But you can't become a rabbi just because you want to. You had to be chosen by the richest and most influential members of the community. It was their decision, and there were many boys with ambitions to become a rabbi. There was nothing about Srully that would appeal to the elite. He blushed when he spoke in public. He didn't have a good voice. He was skinny, short, and stooped. He was not a good speaker. It wasn't enough to be devout, you had to be able to communicate your message, you had to be able to make the Torah readings come alive and arouse feelings of piety in the faithful.

Srully was very religious, but above all else, he loved books. The beauty of the books. The way in which the words of the holy scriptures resonated with him. He loved to ask questions, to try to understand, to see connections, to search for meaning, to find it and lose track of it again, and to search for answers over and over again. And then, being a rabbi meant devoting yourself to the community. It was a heavy responsibility, more onerous than being head of a family. To answer to this one and that, to solve problems people had, however large or small, to resolve disputes or settle quarrels between husband and wife, among neighbours and among brothers and cousins. Disagreements had existed since Cain and Abel and ended very badly, he had read these tales so often that it was enough to scare him off. You had to settle people down, steer them in the right direction, find solutions, provide advice, approval and guidance, and impose order. And the very worst obligation, it occurred to Srully, was that if he became a rabbi, he would have to represent the community at City Hall.

Just thinking about it made him unbearably anxious. Srully didn't like any of those things, he just liked studying. Thinking and studying. He loved chanting. Whispering the scriptures until his throat was dry from repeating the same words, the same passages, sometimes until he was in a trance. At his age, he was among those who knew the greatest number of lines of the Torah by heart. He was one of the best at discussing the most obscure teachings of the Talmud.

But only in small groups.

He liked being in a small study group, even with a scholar from New York or elsewhere, two or three people at most, with the scriptures open in front of them. In less than a second, he could locate the right quotation to support an argument or fuel a discussion, and that's what he liked. Finding a line of reasoning, an answer – that was his passion. He liked to argue, expound, find a satisfactory solution and sometimes reach a state of enlightenment, a point at which you are so happy that it takes your breath away. He would savour these rare moments of bliss knowing that the next day or even the next minute he would have to start all over again.

He liked all of that. He loved it with all his heart.

But to go as far as stepping up onto the *bimah*, speaking to the congregation about what he had learned with so much joy and so much effort, proclaiming in a loud and intelligible voice what he considered to be the truth, when the truth was actually so subtle and so variable, that terrorized him and scared him to death.

Srully was born and raised on Hutchison Street, very close to Bernard, where he still lived. He had been going to the *yeshiva* at the corner of Saint-Viateur, one block from his house, since he was twelve years old. It is probably true to say that in seven years, if you take account of the fact that he came home at lunchtime and returned to the *yeshiva* after supper, he had travelled the length of Hutchison between Bernard and Saint-Viateur at least 21,330 times. For anyone, even for a boy of his age, dodging tricycles, scooters and bicycles, the trip would normally take one hundred and ten to one hundred and twenty seconds, but for Srully it took just forty-five seconds.

With rounded shoulders and his head bowed, he walked so quickly and hurriedly that any new people in the neighbourhood would be surprised. But the long-time residents, who were so used to the quick gait of the Hasidim, didn't even notice him. They knew that from sundown on Fridays and all day on Saturday, they would slow the pace down considerably, so much so that Hutchison Street would look completely different. The sidewalk became a place of relaxation: men chatted with each other, two, three, four at a time, as they ambled along, young couples walked side by side with smiles on their faces, entire families, pushing baby carriages, walked up and down in their finery, the old folks shooting the breeze, the young ones running up ahead, in keeping with the customs.

In Srully's heart, this wasn't a day of rest. It was far from Shabbat, a blessed day he cherished, not only for the rest, but also for the prayers and chants that were different from the weekday ones. With his entire being in turmoil, Srully was torn apart. He had to answer his mother and he didn't know what to tell her. He had tried, without much success, to explain why he didn't want to get married or become a rabbi, that he only liked to study, which she already knew. If it hadn't been for money problems, his mother would have liked to let him do what he liked and she would even have been proud of him, but things being what they were, with his father slaving away, they had to find a way to make ends meet. It was a terrible dilemma for everyone. The only one who could find a solution was him.

Srully was hungry. When he finished school, he was always very hungry. On a normal day, he would have already been back home in forty-five seconds. He would have washed his hands and said the prayer for handwashing, then another prayer before bolting his meal down, and a final one before going back to his books. Today, he slowed down. If he could, he would have stayed at the *yeshiva*. He was afraid to go home. That very morning, when it was still dark out, his mother had spoken to him in a stricter tone than usual, telling him that the house was getting too small for everyone, that his brothers and sisters were growing up, and that the more the children grew the more room they took and the more food they ate. "And don't forget, Srully, another child will be born in one month, God willing." God help me, he thought, his mother had even phoned a match-maker she knew. "You know, Srully, a young rich girl who could get us out of this bind would be more than welcome." The anxiety machine inside him began to rev up. Praying and chanting had had practically no effect on his situation. What was he going to say to his mother?

When he reached his house, Srully turned right around and ran back to school. He went right to his desk and pulled out the letter that his maternal uncle had sent him, confirming his earlier offer. "Come, Srully," his old uncle had said, "come whenever you like. I have no one left, you will be comfortable, you will be able to study as much as you like. Srully, our community definitely needs young men like you."

When his uncle had first mentioned moving to New York, he had thanked him. Srully kissed his uncle's hand and touched his forehead with it. Then he hugged his uncle. But Srully had no intention of leaving his childhood home. He was happy here, with his family, friends and teachers. Hutchison Street, where he had grown up, was all he knew and loved. He had run up and down his street so much that he had worn out the soles of at least a dozen pairs of shoes, which were often too small. Hutchison was not just his street, but also his universe.

Everything would be different in New York, where he had once spent a week with his uncle. He hadn't liked it. Down there, the *yeshiva*, which was two blocks from his uncle's house, was nearly identical to his own *yeshiva*, but the people who taught there and studied there were not. He had found them full of themselves, conceited about how much they knew, which is not at all what a Hasid should be like, nothing like the Hasids here. Only one thing was better about it – the library. It was bigger, it had more books, and it was full of books he had never read.

Srully's eyes were full of tears as he walked slowly

toward his house with his piece of paper folded up and clenched in his right hand. He had made his decision. He didn't have a choice. He would go to New York.

His heart was beating so hard that it hurt. He wasn't hungry any more.

FRANÇOISE CAMIRAND

Srully. She had watched little Srully grow up. What a pleasure it was to rediscover him, to get into the head of the passionate, anguished, solitary young man he had become. As a child, he had looked like the other boys, but, around the age of twelve, he had changed. She didn't see him every day, but each time she did, she noticed the difference. He was always sitting on the front steps with his nose in a book, oblivious to the outside world. While the other boys were racing around on their bicycles, kibitzing with one another, or just hanging out together, he would be walking alone, holding a book in his hand.

She was reluctant to enter Srully's world, just as she was afraid to penetrate the entire universe of the Hasidic Jews, which seemed so mysterious to her. Then one day, she set aside her fears: ready or not, here I come, one, two, three, go! I'm diving in, I don't have a choice. That started the ball rolling.

Right away, she felt a bond between herself and Srully. In a split second. Her own love of books had something to do with this breakthrough. What they had in common was much more striking than their differences.

The connection dawned on her spontaneously and words came easily to her. She was always delighted to write about Srully, her twin from another life, if only because they shared a desire to do what they loved and were driven by a similar passion.

Emboldened by her feat of having made Srully come to life in her book, she began to think about the old Hasidic woman who had always fascinated and touched her. Well before she began her Hutchison Street project, she had thought about writing a short story about her.

She grabbed her handbag and went out. She wanted to refresh her memory and to feel once more the chord the woman had struck in her.

The lady she called Batsheva the Grandmother lived on the Mile End side of the street about six or seven houses down from her place. Françoise walked south toward Saint-Viateur with her heart racing and her head abuzz with words and emotions.

She saw her on the sidewalk in front of her house, surrounded by children. This was the first time she had seen her standing outside.

Two young twelve-year-olds were gently propping her up on either side, each one taking her arm and helping her climb the steps of her concrete staircase. Françoise slowed down and looked at them. There was no rush, everything was smooth and slow, as if the kids were carrying a tray of crystal glasses that they were trying hard not to drop. Were these her grandchildren or great-grandchildren?

Françoise went as far as Saint-Viateur and then turned around and came back. The old lady was already indoors, settled into her armchair and looking out onto the street. Children, younger than the ones who had helped her up the stairs, were playing on the sidewalk.

As Françoise walked along, she repeated her mantra: give me good words, the right words, let me slip subtly into the body, the head, and the heart of this woman I have seen so often, peering out of the left corner of her window. Give me good words, the right words ... easy does it ...

Françoise walked home and went up to her office. Taking her time, with the mantra still bouncing around in her head, she wrote the story of Batsheva the Grandmother. From beginning to end, nearly all in one go.

BATSHEVA THE GRANDMOTHER

She spent her days sitting by the picture window, perched in its left-hand corner. From there, she could see the outside staircase and a stretch of sidewalk where the little ones played and where the bigger kids waited for the school bus. She sat in a comfortable easy chair. In the early morning, well before her great-grandchildren left for school, Batsheva was already there, looking out, her hands folded over her bony midriff. She couldn't see very well anymore, she could hear almost nothing, she didn't eat much, she wasn't a good sleeper, but her heart was holding up. That heart of hers had seen much worse. Batsheva had lived through the most terrible atrocities the world has ever seen, but much later she had also witnessed the most beautiful things that life has to offer.

She never talked about it. She had never talked about it. What good would it do? And, in any case, how could you possibly talk about the unspeakable?

She didn't talk about the good things either. All the people who had lived through good times with her were still alive, thank God. Why would she talk to them about things they were already aware of?

In the early years, of course, the old folks had also lived through poverty and misery. But why remind yourself? Everything was over and forgotten.

Poverty and misery, they're nothing. They are part of life.

The unspeakable is not part of life. She had never thought that the unspeakable was part of life.

In the history of her people, the unspeakable had occurred several times over. Her mind was too weary to remember all the countries where this had happened. She didn't want to remember, she wanted to cleanse her heart before she died.

She prayed. Several times a day, she prayed for it never to happen again. Not in her lifetime, or in the lifetime of any other human being.

For years, she had managed to forget everything. Forever, she thought.

When she came to this country, she lived with distant relatives who had welcomed her with great generosity. She would get so tired from working all day that she would fall dead asleep. The house was filled to the rafters with people – uncles, aunts, cousins big and small – and there was a lot to do. And there were always newcomers showing up, people who had escaped, like her, thank the Lord. Everyone squeezed in as best they could. They prayed a lot and ate very little.

Then she got married. And children began to arrive.

She had six of them, may God bless them and keep them in good health, along with their children and their grandchildren. She used to be so exhausted that the sound of a baby crying was the only thing that could wake her up at night. Nights were too short, but she didn't have dreams or nightmares, thank God. The alarm would go off in the early hours of the morning, and she would be off and running again. Hand-washing, prayers, breakfast for everyone, making do with clothes that were not warm enough and boots in need of repair. After the children left, she would fall asleep. But not for long. She didn't have a washing machine back then and washed clothes by hand. She had to clean house, make meals when the cupboards were bare, and prepare for Shabbat and all the other holidays without two nickels to rub together. She had to mend and sew and iron and scrub the entire house. And scrimp and save. They were penniless and she would have to boil her soup bones over and over again.

Batsheva had never enjoyed good health. She sometimes wondered how she had managed to survive and make it to old age. She never complained. That was all part of life. She had seen so very much when she was young … It's nothing, all of that, hardship, work, fatigue, poverty and even misery and illness, it's all part of life.

She had reached old age and she couldn't hope for a better way to end her life. All her children were married; they had children and grandchildren. None of them was hard-up. Quite the opposite. And they were all in good health.

What more could she ask for at the end of her life?

"Peace ... Soon I will die peacefully ..."

Then everything that she wanted to forget started coming back. In the middle of the night. Always the same images, night after night. Her brothers and her sisters forcibly snatched from their beds, carried off like animals to the slaughter, while she hid. She watched them being beaten but she couldn't cry out. She would sit bolt upright in bed, trembling and in a sweat. She hoped that her screams had stayed inside of her, that she hadn't woken anyone up. It doesn't help to cry out anymore. She should have done so long ago. She should have stopped them. She should have grabbed the murderous hands. She should have screamed loud enough for God to hear. She was crying now. She had never seen her brothers and sisters again. She cried her heart out. Some nights, the dreams were so vivid that she would get up and go looking for her brothers and her sisters all over the house. She would open the door of the apartment and go down the stairs. She had to find them.

Her son or daughter-in-law would catch her in time, before she reached the sidewalk. They would speak to her in soothing tones and gently walk the Grandmother back to her room.

When that happened, she would be exhausted for many long hours. It began to happen more and more often, despite her prayers. She would even feel weary sitting by the window and watching the children.

Batsheva the Grandmother wanted nothing more than

to die peacefully, giving thanks to God. She didn't want to die with screams caught in her throat, images spinning in her head, hatred lodged in her heart, because that way the unspeakable would have got the best of her, in the same way that it had annihilated her brothers and sisters and millions of other people.

When it happened, she would carry the entire world on her frail shoulders – victims, executioners and witnesses all tangled up together. She would reach out to them with her aching body. And the question that had been inscribed in her DNA since the first time the Jews were exiled would come back to break her heart. Why? Why? Why? And she would be afraid. Terribly afraid.

She prayed that the human race would never again …
And she prayed.
To forget. To die in peace.
And she prayed.
She prayed.

Hutchison is a Scottish name. Montreal changed the name of Taylor Street to Hutchison to honour the family that had sold its land to the city. That was back in 1889.

Hutchison Street stretched northward as the city expanded out from the river at the southernmost end, and gradually became what it is today. Saint-Viateur Street, built in 1896, was named in honour of the Clerics of Saint Viator, a teaching order based in Outremont. Bernard Avenue did not get its name until 1912.

Hutchison is a street like no other. The proof? Ask any taxi driver, whether he has just arrived in Montreal or has lived here for generations. Ask him where Hutchison Street is, or better still, give him an address and let him drive you there. No driver will say that he doesn't know where it is, no one will make you repeat the name, and no one will get lost.

Hutchison has always had one sidewalk in Mile End and the other in Outremont. Feet spread apart, caught between two stools like the many immigrants who live in the neighbourhood. The street is none the worse for it. Even after the municipal upheaval, a project called *Une île une ville*, when Montreal was reorganized into boroughs – *arrondissements* – Hutchison Street remained split down the middle. One side landed in the borough of Plateau-Mont Royal, the other in Outremont. Not only does it have a double affiliation along the east-west axis, but it is cut twice along the north-south, by Mont-Royal Boulevard in the south and by the railway line that intersects Hutchison just past Van Horne Avenue further north.

From Sherbrooke Street to the Jean-Talon train station, which used to double as the Parc metro station, Hutchison appears and disappears several times. It never runs in a straight line the way streets often do in Montreal. Unusually erratic, the street changes direction several times, becoming one-way north, or one-way south, and unexpectedly two-way from Fairmount to Van Horne. Speed bumps are now built into the roadway and in the summertime large flower planters are installed right in the middle of the road on the stretch between Laurier and Van Horne.

At first sight, Hutchison looks like many other residential streets in Montreal with its two- or three-storey row housing, brick or grey stone facades, outside staircases that are either straight or spiral, balconies, postage-stamp gardens of dirt, grass or flowers, lots of trees and few restaurants or stores. The exterior architecture has not changed much. Except that the wood and wrought iron on some of the staircases and balconies have been replaced with more modern materials that need less maintenance.

The corner of Hutchison and Bernard, on the Mile End side, has undergone the most change since 1970. An immense restaurant painted in an improbable Mediterranean blue, which violated the French language law, Bill 101, by displaying the English name "Buy More," replaced a vacant lot, on which a single gas pump had stood alongside the semblance of a garage. With time, the guy who was nicknamed Monsieur Buy More grew tired of flipping burgers and skewering souvlaki. He rented out the restaurant and then, a few years later, he sold the building, including the second floor, to the neighbourhood Hasidic Jews.

After the building changed hands, all the windows were papered over, and the premises seemed to have been abandoned. Then, bit by bit, the place at the corner became a gathering spot, although the dirty and yellowing paper was not removed. The building was going to be turned into a synagogue, no doubt, with a school on the top floor. It would not have been the first time in the neighbourhood, where as far back as the 1980s a huge rooming house with furnished 1½ apartments, on the corner of Hutchison and Saint-Viateur, had been demolished and a synagogue and *yeshiva* erected on the lot. It was the first one on the street, or at least the most visible because of its size and the number of Hasidim who used it every day and not just on Shabbat or on holidays. A few years ago, it even made headlines along with the neighbour it backed on to, the Park Avenue YMCA.

The houses on Hutchison Street have stayed pretty much the same. The occupants have come and gone, although some people have lived there for decades. The gradual increase in the Hasidic population is the most obvious change. It's crystal clear when you see the number of children playing in the streets, and the synagogues, the *yeshivot*, the *mikvaot* and the *mezuzot* proliferating before your very eyes. That's what makes Hutchison Street so unique, a street split between Mile End and Outremont. Between Yaveh, God, Allah ... or none of the above.

THE OUTREMONT SIDE

THE DIARY OF HINDA ROCHEL

I said to my mother, "I would like to write a book one day, when I grow up." I don't know why I said it. I must have been out of my mind, for sure. She didn't know what I was talking about. The only book she knows is the Torah. She must have read other books in school. But never secular books like I have. She stopped going to school after fourth grade. When she finally understood what I was saying, she sighed. She raised her eyes to the heavens and looked at me as if I had just landed from another planet. When you have children, she said, you won't have time for anything else anymore. She didn't ask me whether I wanted to get married and have children. You don't ask a question like that in our community. Everyone gets married. The only non-married people I know are my Uncle Shmully, who is crippled, and an aunt of Naomi's, who is very weird and who set their house on fire. In the end, my mother uttered the same words she always does when I ask her something a little bit different. She said, in an angry tone of voice, "My dear daughter, a woman must get married, she must have children and bring them up, she is NOT supposed to read and write!"

As if I didn't know that already. Sometimes I just want to. May Hashem forgive me, I want to. I don't know what to do about her anymore. She just ... no, I can't write that down in my diary.

CHAWKI AND ISABELLE

Ever since he had read Andrea Camilleri's novels in French translation, Chawki had started using the word *coucourde* instead of *tête* to refer to his head. Isabelle had read the same books, and when they talked to each other they used expressions like *pirsonnellement en pirsonne*, and many other mangled forms of French that made them laugh. *Coucourde* came up the most often in their conversations because Chawki's own *coucourde* gave him a lot of trouble. It came unscrewed and then got screwed back together again fifty times a day. Well, not that many times, but Chawki tended to exaggerate – exaggeration was part of his Arabic background – although he actually felt that way, and it was *his* head.

His quirky head would shed a dim, gloomy light on something that had seemed crystal clear and cheery only seconds before, turning it into a murky, mushy mess. His mood was like a light bulb that can be switched on and off. Over the course of a day, however, the light bulb would stay switched on longer than it was switched off. But why did it go off so suddenly and turn back on inexplicably when, objectively, nothing around him had changed?

For a few seemingly endless minutes, everything would be ugly and incomprehensible, and everything in the world that he was most attached to would suddenly appear wishy-washy and worthless. Nothing meant anything anymore. Everything was scrambled in his *coucourde*, and he would question everything: his life, his decisions, and even his love for Isabelle.

And then, bang, a cheerful mood would sweep over him in a miraculous and totally random way.

"How can the same life, on the same day, be either deadly boring or absolutely splendid?" he would ask when he came back to his senses. Sometimes he wondered where the truth lay. Was it in his moments of light? Or in his moments of darkness?

Since he was unable to answer these agonizing questions with any certainty, he tried not to think about them too much.

Chawki had met Isabelle when they were both studying in Paris. He loved her from the moment he laid eyes on her. She had begun to love him nearly a month later. Soon after that month, which had seemed like an eternity to him, they promised to love each other forever and set a date to get married. They had to leave enough time for Isabelle's parents, who had never crossed the ocean before, to make the necessary arrangements to attend their daughter's wedding. Chawki didn't have any family left. His relatives had all been killed in brutal tribal warfare. Hate and vengeance had prevailed for generations.

He was the sole survivor of his immediate family.

Chawki and Isabelle had been married for twenty years and were still as much in love with one another as they had been at the start. Their love had never stopped growing. In fact, it had deepened and multiplied by three — three children they adored. Their marriage was what would be called a mixed marriage, since he was Tunisian and she Québécoise. But aren't marriages always mixed, formed as they are of two individuals with different personalities?

And different they were. She was blond with translucent skin. She was slim and almost as tall as Chawki, who was of average height, rather stocky, with dark skin and curly hair. She wanted Chawki to teach the children Arabic, but he wanted to forget all about his language and culture. She insisted on giving them Arabic names even if they didn't speak their father's language, although he didn't see the point. She wanted to go on a trip to Tunisia, whereas he was far more interested in Mexico.

Isabelle didn't understand. She said to him, "Why are you so stubborn? Why are you denying who you are?" "But I'm not," he replied, "how could I deny who I am? And even if I wanted to ... All of that is over. Keeping the past alive is like trying to feed a corpse. Even though I have given the name Fathi to my son, he will never look like his grandfather. His grandfather is dead and I almost died. If I hadn't fled, I would never have met you. Why pretend? Why try to mumble a few words in a language I know my children will never speak correctly?

To be "cute," as the English say, to be exotic? Let's leave the dead with the dead and take care of the living instead. The past will never come to life again. I prefer to take care of the present. And don't forget, dear, that for the Buddhists, identity is just another illusion."

Words, words, Isabelle would hum to herself … From time to time, she would bring it up again and Chawki would respond in pretty much the same way. But she couldn't understand. His answers didn't make sense. It's one thing not to want to live in the past, but it's another to completely erase it just to take care of the present, as he claimed. The wheels in your *coucourde* are not turning well, my love.

She didn't dare talk to him about losing his family and his country. The subject was off limits.

Chawki, as he said himself, wanted to take care of the present, and the day-to-day. And he did a great job. It was part of his charm and it was among the many things she loved about him. He was the only man she knew who was so attached to the little things in life. He knew how to make the most of every minute. He would conjure up these moments, which he did his best to cherish. He was a magician of everyday life. With him, it was impossible to be bored. In this family, you would never hear a child say: oh no, not hamburgers again! He was almost always the one who put the meals together. He could even turn leftovers into a feast. Isabelle was delighted. Cooking was not her strong suit, but when it came to eating, watch out! She could certainly hold her own. She was good-looking, and he adored cooking for her. When he was preparing the meals, he would picture her closing her eyes in order to taste the food better. He imagined her loving eyes opening and gazing at him as he watched her. You could never tell what would happen next. She might gobble her food down, without saying anything, like their favourite character, Montalbano, or she might babble away and ask incessant questions. "Eat, my dear, it's going to get cold. I'll tell you how I made it after." But he never did tell her because afterward he couldn't remember. The present had already passed.

His children weren't always as enthusiastic about his cooking, but when their friends came over and when they all gathered around the table to stuff their faces, he would become the coolest father of them all.

Cooking was the only part of his native Tunisia that he wanted to keep alive. He knew how to make almost all the dishes he had once eaten, and he did so by heart. And he would make up recipes for the ones he had forgotten about. He never opened a cookbook and he would never set foot in a Tunisian or other North African restaurant.

He wasn't Tunisian anymore, and he was only Québécois out of love for Isabelle and his children. He loved this country because he loved them. They say that a friend of a friend is also your friend, and he would say — and he really meant it — "the country of my love is my country." Love had been his gateway to this country and its culture. It had been a red carpet that is not necessarily rolled out for all immigrants.

He had lost both his family and his homeland in one fell swoop, and he knew that his love for Isabelle, and then for his children, had given him a new lease on life.

When the light in his *coucourde* dimmed, and his love for Isabelle and his children shone less brightly, he felt like an orphan. He was unhappy. But it came back, his love always came back even stronger.

If Isabelle ever fell out of love with him one day — which was unimaginable, unthinkable — he didn't know whether he would be able to survive another loss.

We will never know exactly what happened in Chawki's *coucourde* for his attitude to change so radically from one day to the next — toward his past, his identity, his culture, and his language. Had he finally come to terms with the tragic events that had dogged him for so long? Was it the impact of 9/11, which made people look at Muslims — and even those who looked like they might be Muslims — as if they were all terrorists? Was it the questions of his children that forced him to think about who he was? "Are we Arabs, Papa? At school, everyone is saying bad things about Arabs. Are we Muslims, Papa, are we terrorists?" He answered them as best he could. "I am a Muslim because of my parents and my upbringing. I was a Muslim for the first twenty-five years of my life. Bless those who are still Muslim, may they live in peace. I'm not a Muslim anymore. I'm not religious. At the moment, you, children, are not Catholic or Muslim. When you're old enough, you will choose, if you wish. Leave the disagreements, disputes and hatred to other people. You are the new citizens of the world. Like so many other people, you come from a mixed family, a broad-minded one without fanaticism, which embraces all difference. But good lord, we are living in Quebec, which is, as far as I know, a free country, open to the world!"

And so it was that, in the wake of September 11th, without being pressured into it by Isabelle, Chawki began talking to his children about his youth in Tunisia, about the life of the grandparents they had never heard anything about. He also began looking for some way to teach them Arabic. He didn't really know how to go about it, or where to begin, but he started by browsing through a few bookstores in Ville Saint-Laurent. Then he discovered that the Mile End library, which was just a stone's throw away from his house, had a shelf full of children's books in Arabic, along with CDs for learning the language, and CDs of Arabic music. He had all the resources he needed close at hand.

Isabelle had been waiting for this for a long time. She was overjoyed. The children, on the other hand, were not so thrilled. They loved their father's stories, and begged for more, but learning the language was another matter. They grumbled at the start of every lesson. And yet, whenever they learned a new word, they were proud of themselves. They went straight to their mother to practise it, until she, too, began to speak a bit of broken Arabic like they did. Chawki found it hard going. Every week, he would spend one hour with the eldest and an hour and a half with the two younger kids, not counting all the time he spent between lessons reviewing the words they had already learned to make sure they were sticking in their *coucourdes*.

As for his own head, the *coucourde* that played so many tricks on him, it sometimes went dark on him, but less and less often. It would leave him alone to horse around with his kids, to tease them. The children struggled to produce the guttural sounds of the sacred Arabic language. They didn't always manage, but it was fun to try. They laughed a lot. It brought them closer together and was well worth the effort. "Why on earth didn't I start earlier?"

When life at the office became too stressful for her, Isabelle would slip away so that she could be at home *pirsonnellement en pirsonne* for the hilarious shenanigans. She was tickled pink, in seventh heaven, ecstatic – even though she had to do more cooking now that Prof. Chawki had begun to take his role so seriously. Yet, she had never before heard him laugh with as much gusto – a real belly laugh, finally.

THE DIARY OF HINDA ROCHEL

We kids cannot go into our parents' bedroom. It is forbidden, and we know that. You just never do it. One time, the door was left open and I saw two beds with a small night table between them. In five or six years, I will also have a bed next to a man I don't know. Sometimes, I look forward to it. Sometimes, I don't. I know that a man and a woman make babies together. But I don't know how they do it. "It's natural," my mother told me. "You will do what your husband asks. A woman must obey her husband." I tried to find out what my husband might ask me to do. My little brother began to cry and my mother ran over in a flash to look after him. I saw it on her face. She was happy. My mother doesn't like to lie, I know her well. When she doesn't know what to say, she prefers not to say anything.

Women don't study the Talmud and that's why they have to obey, that's what my cousin Srully told me. I was little then but I have a very good memory. I am beginning to understand. Women have to obey because they cannot study. But when I think about, I am still puzzled. I like to study. I want to study. I don't understand anything at all. No, I don't.

FRANÇOISE CAMIRAND

On the radio someone is introducing the latest book written by a well-known writer. He is telling a bit of the story.

The host asks, "Is it true, is it about him?"

The commentator replies, "No, it's not about him. He never makes himself one of the characters in his own books. But it's good, very good."

The host replies, "But I like to read a true story. It has to be well written, of course, but a true story, you know, it's something special ..."

The commentator says, "We often tend to confuse actual events and the fictional narrative. In Germani's novel, we enter into a world that he has created. It's credible and we believe in it, it's true because we believe it. And it's well written, that's what's important, basically. It's amazingly well written, and it exudes truth."

The radio discussion she happened to tune into while waiting for the news to come on made her think about what her publisher Jean-Hugues had told her, when he tried to convince her to write her autobiography. "Your readers want to get to know you," he had told her. "They are waiting impatiently. You know how popular true stories are these days. Everyone wants true stories. Literature is crazy at the moment. Just say that it's a true story and it will sell like hotcakes. Are readers fed up with fiction, or what? Have readers become warped by all the outrageous true confessions they get from the stars and by all the reality shows they see on television? Is fact more thrilling than fiction? Are writers just on an ego trip, forgetting about their readers? Even in the movies, you see the subtitle "true story," sometimes in bigger letters than the actual film title. I'm flabbergasted by this appetite for true stories. And yet, mysteries sell very well, too, and you couldn't get more fictional than that."

She listens to the news until the end of the broadcast. She turns the radio off and puts on a CD of Corsican music. It takes just a few seconds for her office to be filled with the sounds of singing voices. The plants and cats are happy, and so is she.

She fills a pot with water and puts it on for tea. She is thinking about the character she is working on. She imagines the character hunched over an open book, a large book which she is reading zealously, standing up while making tea, just like she is. There's no noise in the house now, except for the fridge that hums occasionally, but she doesn't hear it, just as she doesn't notice the burbling of the water. A strange noise penetrates the silence. She glances up, startled, and looks around. She had forgotten where she was. There is not a drop of water left in the pot and the bottom is burned.

The first time she saw her was at the bookstore called L'Écume des Jours, on Saint-Viateur. Clearly, this woman is in love with books. At the Olimpico Café, right across the street from the bookstore, she unwraps what she has just bought. She looks at the books from all angles, strokes them and, with a smile, mulls over which one she will dive into first.

Over the years, Françoise has met her in the bookstore or at the coffee shop from time to time. When she saw her at the drugstore a couple of days ago, Françoise realized that she had not seen her in a long time.

The person she would end up calling Martine Saint-Amant had changed a lot. Her face was pale and wrinkled and she didn't look at all well. She looked nothing like the lively woman she had noticed a few months earlier. It was as if she were gripping her book to avoid falling, her hands trembling ever so slightly. She was sitting down, waiting for her prescription to be filled.

She was so absorbed in reading her book that she didn't hear her name being called. The pharmacist repeated her name a bit louder. The other customers indicated that they weren't the ones whose name was being called, and still she didn't move. Françoise went up to her and gently touched her arm, "Madame, I think it's your turn." The detective book addict looked as if she had been woken up from a long sleep. As the woman got up, Françoise glanced over and had the time to note that she was reading Michael Connelly's *The Poet*, which is an excellent crime novel.

MARTINE SAINT-AMANT

She read to escape.

From the time she woke up until the minute she fell asleep, and sometimes in the middle of the night when she couldn't sleep, she read detective novels. It was the only kind of book that she could stand, the only thing she was able to do. She was captivated by crime fiction, which gave her pleasure, gave her the impression of travelling and allowed her to stop thinking about what had happened to her.

Reading was the only thing she had found to offset the crushing weight of her pain.

She read while lying on the living room couch, sitting at the kitchen table and sipping a coffee or nibbling on something, reclining amid cushions and pillows in her bedroom, soaking in her bath, or ensconced in an easy chair in her TV room with the television turned off. She even read when she went to the bathroom. But never in her office, or her husband's office.

She read while waiting for things to blow over.

Before she became a detective book addict, wandering from room to room to find a new position and to rest her eyes, Martine Saint-Amant used to work in a very nice communications firm downtown. She was not the type to be outdone, and she worked flat out in order to compete with the young go-getters who were breathing down her neck. She overextended herself so much that she snapped. She had a burn-out. On doctor's orders, she went on stress leave and took time off to rest. They said "burn-out" in the workplace instead of depression, making it sound more exotic and less like a mental illness. If you were burned out, it simply meant that your motor was burned out from working your butt off. You had bust your ass for the company, so much so that you could pat yourself on the back and boast about what you had accomplished.

Good things come in pairs, as the expression goes. They also say that it never rains but it pours. Her husband left her the same week. It didn't come out of the blue, it had been building up for a long time. She had been living with her husband, her second husband actually, for nearly ten years, and she had wanted to be with him forever.

She was back to square one, an expression that used to make her smile at one time.

Martine Saint-Amant had always been an avid reader. She was passionate about books. Since she was a little girl, reading had been not just her favourite pastime, but her daily bread. Even after a day at the office, when she came home feeling tired and harried, she always found the time and energy to read, if only a few pages. She would read all sorts of things, but especially the intense, deep and questioning novels that unsettle all your ideas. She liked the sometimes painful experience of diving deep into her soul by reading the work of writers who were spilling their guts, who were tearing their hearts out to try to find the meaning of life with words that were infinitely beautiful, almost poetic. The meaning of her own life had just been seriously toppled, which meant that she could no longer open that kind of book without feeling nauseous. She had enough turmoil in her own life. She didn't need to add any more. The slightest nudge, or any further emotion, would push her over the edge.

But she missed reading. The act of reading, and the object, too. She liked knowing that a book was waiting for her, for you are never alone knowing that there's a good book waiting. Reading in any old place, at any time, in any position, without making any noise, without bothering anyone. She loved to hug the rectangular pile of pages pressed one against the other, with many words written black on white, and sail away on uncharted waters, exploring herself or other people. When she was little, she used to say, "I like reading too much." Now that she was grown up, the "too much" had stuck with her.

Before her infatuation with detective novels, she had read one or two books by Agatha Christie, one or two by Simenon. She had liked them, but she was not hooked. And then one day, a miracle happened. About two weeks had gone by since her husband had left her, since she had quit her job, and since her girlfriends had gone back to work after paying her a couple of visits of support. Home alone in her Hutchison Street condo, her eyes were puffy and red, she felt weak and defeated, and she had no appetite. She was going around in circles, all by herself. She was at loose ends, and she didn't know what to do with her life. She rummaged through her bookcases looking for a book to distract her a bit. The screenwriters for *Desperate Housewives* would have had trouble filling five minutes of air time with Martine Saint-Amant, who was just a shadow of her former self, much too dull, as her mother might have said, but she wasn't there to comfort her because, "Mascouche, you know, isn't a stone's throw away from Montreal, not when the car is in the garage because your father got into an accident, and anyway, if you would only stop crying, dear, a good-for-nothing like him isn't that hard to replace, anyways ..."

The anti-depressants were not working. She felt a continual upheaval inside her chest, as if she were being sliced into strips by a razor. Each sharp blade had a colour and texture of its own, and quivered in a different way. She had spent ten years of her life with him. At first, they were crazy about each other. Then their relationship grew deeper, then more laid back. They vowed they would grow old together, until all hell broke loose. "What did I do to deserve this?" She got no relief, even with the antidepressants and anti-anxiety meds.

A miracle occurred when a friend left a book at her place – *Have Mercy On Us All* by the French crime writer Fred Vargas. It was love at first sight. During the long hours she spent with Chief Inspector Jean-Baptiste Adamsberg and Captain Adrien Danglard she didn't feel any pain. She felt great. She began to regain some of the concentration that had gone missing for quite some time. Even before she finished reading the book, she rushed to the Mile End library to take out everything she could find about the *Commissaire*'s investigations. Then she got into Harry Bosch, then Kurt Wallander, and more.

Little by little, she became detached from real life and immersed in the world of crime fiction. She was particularly interested in the people who investigated the crimes: inspectors, lieutenants, detectives, sergeant-detectives, private eyes, captains, chief inspectors, depending on the book she was reading. The authors didn't really matter much to her. She was more interested in the protagonists – and sometimes their partners. She soon forgot that these characters had been invented by someone who was an author. She became attached to Bosch, Erlendur, Montalbano, John Rebus, Frédéric Fontaine, Wallander, Adam Dalgliesh, Varg Veum, Victoria I. Warshawski, Harry Hole, Jessica Balzano, Kevin Byrne, Jack Reacher, Easy Rawlins, Scuder, Pepe Carvalho and so many others.

Each of these detectives, who knocked themselves out trying to track down the guilty party, became closer to her than a brother or a friend. She followed their movements step by step through moments of discouragement, hope or jubilation. For hundreds of pages and during the countless hours she spent reading, she accompanied the detectives just as they kept her company. Sometimes she forgot that she was reading. She was so engrossed in the story that her heart would skip a beat whenever the plot took an exciting or alarming turn.

For her, a detective novel portrayed real life in all its horror and beauty. Perhaps even more than the books she had read before. In those books, life was packaged and edited by the author, but these just described the ordinary life of a guy or sometimes a woman who were just doing their job. Life unfolded with its problems and questions, without any pretence of revolutionizing literature, and yet there would be some passages that took your breath away. The only difference between fiction and real life was that in these books you ended up knowing who was guilty. Yes, that was the good part, you knew who was guilty, but in detective novels that also meant that you had finished reading the book. What she found most exciting was getting there. She loved the ups and downs and the surprises along the way.

Before falling in love with detective novels, she had thought they were all of the same quality. She wouldn't have admitted it, but she once had a certain disdain for this type of writing. When she discovered the hidden jewels of some masterpiece, she was bowled over. It reminded her of something Quebec singer Félix Leclerc had once said about ignorance breeding contempt.

Detective novels, like all literary genres, ranged in quality. Some of them had glaring errors, inconsistencies, sloppy style, but she didn't give a damn. If she didn't know the detective yet, if she wasn't yet attached to him, she would put the book aside and reach for another one. On the other hand, the more she got to know the main character, the more she would disregard flaws in the plot or the writing style the same way you would forgive the faults of a friend, because you know he will come back to his senses, and be the same person you knew and loved. She knew what would happen, so she always had a stack of books waiting for her. The Mile End library was well stocked, the librarians were very nice, and the library itself was only minutes from home. There were also four bookstores, including a used bookshop on Saint-Viateur.

When she started a new book, a new adventure with a detective she was familiar with, she was just as exhilarated as if she was going to meet a lover she hadn't seen for a long time.

Even though she didn't think about it all the time, she was aware of the fact that crime fiction had saved her life. It had at least dragged her out of the quicksand into which she had been sinking for several months. Each mystery distracted her from her personal quest, gave her some respite from herself, gave her the time to rest and the time to heal.

She could experience emotional upheaval and return to her own life at any time while she was reading. A father who found his son again, a mother who was looking for her child, or a mere thank you, a tender gesture of recognition. It could be the emotion of the detective as he came to terms with so much horror, with his powerlessness and his fatigue. It could be anything. She didn't know and she didn't ask questions. She would feel her throat tighten. She would stop right in the middle of a sentence and she would cry, cry, cry, without knowing for whom or for what reason. With her left hand, she would rest the open book on her chest — most of the time she used to read lying down — and with her right hand placed over her eyes, she would continue to sob. Then she would wave her hand around trying to dry her eyes, as if she was spreading face cream over her entire face and as if the lotion were made of salt water. And, without changing positions, without feeling sorry for herself and asking "why, dear God, why," she would start reading again, the way a drunk reaches for his glass, or a druggie takes a toke or shoots up, to try to escape the unbearable just a bit.

FRANÇOISE CAMIRAND

Procrastination. A word that's hard to pronounce. Marcel Proust borrowed it from English, and then popularized it when he made it one of the primary themes of *In Search of Lost Time*. All writers, essayists, script writers and play-wrights are familiar with procrastination, and fall prey to it, except Victor-Lévy Beaulieu, Nancy Huston, Stéphane Laporte, Ismail Kadare, and ... Françoise Camirand.

She never put off till tomorrow what she could do today. Quite the opposite. She did things today which could easily wait until tomorrow. She was a workhorse, with iron discipline, and she worked three hundred days a year, five or six hours a day, sometimes more, without slacking off. Not counting the time she spent reading up on the subject of the book she was working on.

But for the past two or three days, nothing has been the same on Hutchison Street, at least not in Françoise Camirand's study and head. Perhaps it was because she had taken a liking to her long walks through the neighbourhood. She paced and protested like a caged lioness.

She would sit down at her desk, take a peek at her computer, make a face, stand up again, grab a coffee to give her energy, survey her plants and trim them (although there were actually no more yellow leaves to pluck off), drink a cup of tea to stimulate the creative juices, look out the window, put on some music, change CDs, turn it off again, then come back to take another peek at her characters. And then the cycle of coffee, tea, plants and looking out the window would start over again.

She was not her usual self. This had not happened to her for a long time. Even more dangerous, her characters seemed both strange and foreign to her. As if all the affinity, fondness and love she had originally felt for them had dissipated. All at once.

Procrastination was turning into discouragement of the worst kind as she lost sight of the importance of her work. She no longer knew why she was writing. Danger! Handle with care! There were too many bad memories associated with this kind of slump.

She even quarrelled with Jean-Hugues. She got worked up. "It was YOUR idea, not mine. If you want to publish an autobiography, write your own and leave me alone!" He walked out and slammed the door. What babies they were! To be honest, she was taking it out on him. Unhappy with her work, she was looking for a fight. She would have picked a fight with the storekeeper, the mailman, anybody, but he happened to be the one. He talked for the sake of talking, the poor guy, he didn't want to make her do anything. Quite the contrary. He just wanted to talk about Gabrielle Roy's autobiography, *Enchantment and*

Sorrow, which he was rereading, and he had accidentally let slip the idea that Françoise could write her own biography, nothing more. But this wasn't the right time to talk about the past, which she had been struggling with for a few days.

She felt distraught, not so much because of the fight with Jean-Hugues – doors had been slammed many times over the years – but because of the terrible feeling that was weighing her down. She was haunted by her younger days, the time before she began writing ... As if things were floating, as if everything was becoming foreign, as if life no longer had any texture or meaning. It was a state of mind she feared, because she had been there before. It would be so easy to slip into the cycle of self-destruction once again, it would be the next step ... Just because she had changed obsessions, it didn't mean that she was no longer obsessive. She knew what it was like, to let everything go down the toilet.

After Jean-Hugues left, she was still fuming. She had to do something, before everything went to hell in a handcart! She had to break out of her cell immediately. She took her handbag and went out. Around her, the street was teeming with life. It was like a remedy for her, it helped her to put things into perspective, to get her head screwed on straight, to give herself a kick in the ass. Stagnation is a kind of demon. Move, do something! When she was younger, she would have taken a drink, then another and another. But those days were over now.

Drawing inspiration from one of her favourite songs,

Toujours vivant, she decided to grab hold of the lifebuoy.[4] It was a song that celebrated making a mark in this world, never giving up. The words echoed in her head. She just muttered them at first. It was a reflex, she sang without much conviction, but she was soon carried away by the song's ebb and flow. She felt like a fool singing out loud in the middle of the street, but it was a much smaller risk than the one she had just averted. She walked all the way over to Pratt Park, circled it two or three times. She took Fairmount on the way back and rang Jean-Hugues's doorbell.

Since coming to Quebec, his vocabulary had been en-
riched by countless Québécois expressions: words like *ni-
aiser, maganer, achaler … gougoune, moumoune, guidoune*,[5] and
the swearwords so typical of Quebec – all of them related
to religion. And then there were the words specifically
pertaining to winter, like *bancs de neige, sloche, glace noire*
and *poudrerie*.[6] He was a quick learner and he loved the
distinctive flavour of Quebec French. He would say "*tu
m'aimes-tu?*" because he adored Richard Desjardin's song
and found that the repetition of the pronoun *tu* made the
question stronger and more precise. He was able to recognize quality of speech, inventiveness, register and region-
al variations in Quebec French. With time, his ear became
more attuned and he formed certain preferences. Among
his many projects, he planned to publish a collection of
his favourite Quebec terms and expressions, which he
had started jotting down as soon as he arrived in Quebec
in 1975, and even a bit earlier when he fell in love with
a beautiful Quebec woman, whom he had subsequently
followed. He wasn't the following type of guy, but isn't

love a good excuse for changing course?

Jean-Hugues landed in Montreal on the eve of Saint-Jean-Baptiste Day, accompanied by Louise Lavallée, who was doing her doctorate in French literature. It was crazy, it was festive. Montreal appealed to him instantly. Those were heady times in Quebec and its artists were on fire. And he adored artists.

Although Jean-Hugues's love life soon turned sour, and Louise wanted to return to France as soon as possible because she couldn't stand the Québécois, who were country bumpkins in her view, Jean-Hugues decided to stay. He liked the Québécois, whom he found feisty, because for centuries they had resisted and refused to be assimilated by the English majority, and had steadfastly preserved their language and culture. He immediately and wholeheartedly embraced their struggle.

He went home to France to apply for immigration, to see his parents and to finish what he had to finish.

He was twenty-five years old. He was ready for anything and everything, and life in Quebec suited him perfectly, including the cold and interminable winters. Here, he could be what he wanted to be, do what he wanted to do, and become what he wanted to become. The sense of freedom that had prompted him to immigrate was in fact a sense of relaxation. His shoulders loosened up and went back to normal, he became less tight-assed, and his creativity soared.

Although he went back to Europe quite often for work or to see his family in Quimper, in Brittany, he was always happy to come back home to his place on Hutchison Street.

The mantra of the *maudit Français*, which he had heard so often, especially at the beginning, didn't bother him anymore, and sometimes he would use it to make fun of himself or other Frenchmen, or to shut someone up if he didn't like them or wanted to deny them the satisfaction of letting off steam at his expense. He had learned from experience that the tone could be more offensive than the words themselves. If some idiot said to him, "*maudit Français*, go back to where you came from," he would choose between two responses, depending on the person's tone or his own mood. He could say, "go fuck yourself, you asshole" or, a bit more politely, "I chose to live here although I could have gone anywhere else in the world. I came here by choice and for love, can you say as much, you prick?" The other person would say proudly, "Well, I was born here," to which Jean-Hugues Briançon would reply, with the nicest of smiles, "You were born here, so what! We are all born somewhere, but very few people choose their country out of love. You have not chosen your country, but I have. So don't piss me off, and bugger off!"

After the Parti Québécois unexpectedly won the election in November 1976, he was just as happy as the *pure laine* sovereignists who had withstood cold winters for generations, much longer than he had. When Bill 101, the language law, followed, he felt it was important and essential. He thought Quebec needed to include and integrate immigrants in order to become a country.

Little by little, the cliché "they come and steal our jobs" was disappearing from popular opinion and was replaced by "they should at least speak our language if they want to stay here." For Jean-Hugues, learning the language of the country you want to live in was the least you could do. He didn't understand how people could live in a country without being curious about its culture and language, its history and aspirations.

When he first came, he had multiple jobs. He dropped out of his doctorate in linguistics and signed up for a few courses in Quebec literature. He remained optimistic and felt confident that he would find whatever it was he had come looking for. He knew that he would find it, one day. That day came when he met Jean-Marc Gagnon, a crazy young guy with as much ambition as he had, who was as passionate as he was about literature and books. They started their own publishing company. There were lean years, made worse by the departure of Jean-Marc who after eighteen months was fed up with treading water. Jean-Hugues persevered, working as a waiter in a nice café called Aux Gâteries, located a few steps away from the Librairie du Square, a bookstore that was even nicer because of its books and the owner. He stayed the course until he found a manuscript he felt really enthused about. He could sense the author's voice, style and worldview, and he was blown away. That day, he rushed to the telephone even before he had finished reading the book, hoping that the rights were still free.

They were, and so was the novelist. He made an

appointment to meet her that very day.

That was the most beautiful day of his life. He saw a woman with long, light brown hair as lovely as her sparkling eyes. She walked in wearing a long mauve skirt and a bright green tank top. It was summer and her arms were lightly tanned. He had fallen for the book and was now falling head over heels in love with its young author. Thirty years later he could still remember the contrasting colours of her clothes, the way she ran her hands through her hair, and the way she laughed. she was as excited as he was. Perhaps not for the same reasons, but, still, there were sparks between the two of them. He had just read her book and he felt that he already knew her. And yet, after thirty years, there was still something left to discover in her.

Jean-Hugues Briançon's life changed dramatically. Not only had he met the woman of his life, but he had also discovered a novelist whose writing he adored and who would make his little publishing house viable. The novel sold like hotcakes, reaching unexpected sales figures. It was pandemonium in the apartment that doubled as a publishing company, where Jean-Hugues assumed all responsibilities, from CEO to receptionist, including making deliveries by bus, metro or taxi since he didn't yet own a car or have a distributor. He scheduled one interview after another, and also had to reprint the book several times. Not only did the cash drawer begin to fill up for the first time, but his heart throbbed with love. He would sometimes dance around his apartment alone, among the boxes of books. He smoked up his apartment with sage grass that he burned in thanks like indigenous people do, praying for his love to last his whole life.

He didn't yet know how to manage his success, but he was learning quickly. And he had everything to learn. The best thing he already had going for him, hands down, was his love of books and the people who wrote them. Life had given him a chance. His creativity blossomed as he found a way to take full advantage of this gold mine. JHB Éditeur became a respected and prosperous publishing house. JHB worked very hard to ensure that Quebec literature would be read at home, appreciated abroad and translated. A lot of work was involved, and a lot of jet lag. His love of books and writers was equalled only by his good business sense. He had charm, he had a sense of humour and he was persuasive. The *maudit Français* had found his niche.

Since leaving home, he had not moved an inch, he had not left his place on Hutchison Street. It was as if a big change, even one that he had wished for, one that he had chosen, had destabilized him so much that he would spend the rest of his life trying to regain a sense of balance, trying to put roots down. And what better way to anchor yourself than to attach yourself to a woman you love, who loves you, and to engage in fascinating work. When he thought about all the things that life had given him, he felt privileged, grateful and humble.

He lived north of Fairmount, a couple of doors up from La Croissanterie (which had changed names a few times, but which had always remained La

Croissanterie to him, the first café in the neighbourhood to make good espressos). His girlfriend lived on the same street, but further up, between Saint-Viateur and Bernard. Although they had been together for around thirty years, they had never lived together under the same roof. They weren't married and had not had children together. They saw each other several times a week, for business, at his house or at the offices of the publishing company, as well as for pleasure, most of the time at her place. He liked her apartment full of plants and flowers, with the parks of Outremont nearby. He liked to walk with her at his side, crossing the parks and even walking through the cemetery on Mount Royal to get to the mountain. They often had dinner together and sometimes they entertained friends. They would go out to the movies or to see a play, or they would stay at home reading, each of them curled up in an armchair.

The part of the publishing business he liked the best was being the literary editor, even though he actually enjoyed all aspects of the job. In the past thirty years, he had perfected his listening skills, he had learned to ask pointed questions and he had improved his ability to read manuscripts.

Reading the novels of unknown writers, to whom he would respond promptly, with thanks, encouragement and the notes he had made while reading their work, was an important part of his work. He considered it a duty, sometimes a pleasure and even a joy when he discovered a new author.

Reading the latest manuscript of an author he liked, when he knew that the text would become a book in one of the publishing company's series, was a deeply gratifying experience and a delicate one — if the manuscript turned out to be bad, if it turned out that there were serious shortcomings, how could he tell the author tactfully? The pleasure he always derived from discovering a brand new novel would begin with hairs standing up on the back of his neck, and shivers going down his spine. He would disconnect the telephone, then begin reading. He would deploy all his faculties and focus in. He was like an antenna capturing sound waves, a barometer detecting atmospheric conditions. He read lustily all the way through without taking notes. He had a prodigious memory and could talk for hours about books that he loved.

He got up to pour himself a whisky. He sniffed it, picked up the pile of new manuscripts by unknown authors and went out onto his little balcony. It was nice out. He began to daydream. He remembered Françoise's smile and the sly look on her face, "You could be a character in my novel, you live on Hutchison Street too. Readers love true stories, that's what you told me, isn't it?" He had replied, "How sneaky of you, you're now going to talk about me in your novel. Don't forget that I'm your publisher. I have the power of life and death over your manuscript." She had kissed him, after first pinching his arm, her way of showing affection. This was typical, she had been like this since the beginning. "But you are not the only publisher, my crafty fellow." He had brushed his lips against her cheek and whispered, "I am not the only publisher, of course, but I'm the one who's in love with you."

He often used the French term *ma petite vlimeuse*, ever since she had called him *mon ratoureux* one day when they were having a discussion about signing a contract for the screen adaptation of her second novel. When he learned, quite a while later, that the term "*ratoureux*" meant "slick" or "crafty" in Quebec, he sent her an enormous bouquet of flowers with a card addressed to my "*vlimeuse*," which meant essentially the same thing, perhaps with the added connotation of "mischievous." He signed the card "*ratoureusement vôtre*," or "slickly yours." Since then the words "*ratoureux*" and "*vlimeuse*" had become terms of endearment for the two of them.

He wasn't able to concentrate. He was thinking about her, about the characters of Hutchison Street. He suddenly wondered how she would depict him if he did become a character in her novel. It made him smile. He was a bit embarrassed. What would she draw attention to, what would she leave out, and, above all, what part of him would she consider a part of herself? He had often heard her talk about the ties that bound her to her characters and how close she felt to each one of them. He had always marvelled at writing and it was no coincidence that he had become a publisher and literary editor. He had boundless admiration for artists. Art in general and writing in particular had always been a mystery to him. No one had ever been able to demystify the process by which a writer can put a few words together to make a whole that can transport us into another world. A world that we were unaware of just hours earlier. He wondered why he had given up writing himself. He had begun several novels, but hadn't finished a single one. How does someone become a writer, musician, dancer, actor or painter? What accounts for the fact that someone stays on course, despite the challenges, misery, poverty, and lack of recognition and support? Why is it that one person will make it through all that, persist and stay the course, while someone else will give up, and become a publisher or restaurant owner? Was he, Jean-Hugues Briançon, a Frenchman who had been living in Quebec for thirty-three years, a failed writer, as they say about critics, sometimes unfairly? Or rather, could you say that he did not need to define his own existence, fill his existential void, or compensate for his flaws – it doesn't matter what you call it – in this way?

He thought about the way he had lived his life since he decided to start a publishing company. He thought about his friend Jean-Marc, who hadn't been able to hang in there, because his passion for books was not as great. For Jean-Marc, seeing a book hot off the press was not the most beautiful thing in the world, it didn't bring him tremendous joy. How could you overcome all the difficulties if you didn't think it was the most beautiful thing in the world? When he thought about it carefully, he decided that no, he was not a failed writer, but rather a passionate publisher. He was in the right place. And what a place! He had a seat in the front row of literature.

THE DIARY OF HINDA ROCHEL

Today, I received a nice big compliment from Madame Genest. She told me that I was her best student. Not just the best student in the class, but the best one she has ever taught. And Madame Genest is pretty old, so that must add up to a lot of students. She said, "You are a little prodigy, Hinda Rochel." I didn't know what "prodigy" meant. So she said, "My dear child, you have a lot of talent. Do you understand the word 'prodigious' perhaps?" I nodded. "Prodigy is a word in the same family. Look it up in your dictionary."

I was very happy and wanted to repeat Madame Genest's beautiful words to someone. But to whom? No one cares about my life. I'm lucky that I have my diary to write in and that I have *Bonheur d'occasion* to read over again. The more I read that novel, the more I love it. If I had not found it on the sidewalk while walking home from school ...

My mother is calling me.

They never leave me alone. NEVER.

RON KOWALSKI

For him, a three-star hotel room was only one step away from a fleabag room and he went from one to the other as if there was nothing to it. He could sleep in the street or a luxury penthouse, and he did both at regular intervals. He went from one way of life to the other, when he was fed up with one or the other. He didn't make a big deal about it, he didn't feel sorry for himself. Without delay, without fear.

He was not afraid of God or the devil. The only thing that worried him was his own violence.

All his life, he had felt like punching, breaking, hitting, inflicting pain, killing. He had spent his entire life holding back. And he had erased from his memory moments when he had been unable to hold back. Even though he had always felt this violence coursing through his veins, he did not know where it came from, and he wasn't the type to dwell on questions like that.

At school, he controlled himself. He could have killed his teachers, but he had killed no one, he had beaten up barely seven or eight children of his own age. He could have killed them, but he had just injured them. The last time that he injured a classmate, although he had held back just enough not to kill him, he had been permanently expelled from school. When his father found out, he had given him a beating, also controlling himself so that he didn't kill his son, and then he kicked him out of the house. There was no going back. Ron Kowalski was happy. Free at last. No more teachers, no more school principal, no more father. He went to live in the woods. He was happy in the bush, far away from other humans, living with wild animals as his companions. For him, it was the only place where God was not far away. This was God before the Word, this was God as tree, bird, grass, water, sun and moon, a God he wasn't afraid of, whom he loved. But how could he earn any money in the woods?

So he left the forest. And his battles began all over again. Fighting with himself. A ball of pure rage would often form in his stomach.

He was always in a state of alert, ready to lash out at the next person he saw. He always had his fist clenched, his right hand ready to punch and his left hand wrapped around his right to prevent it from doing so.

If the gods of the forest could erase his rage, action could also distract him a bit. He had a talent for moving around, giving himself a sense of importance, selling, buying, inventing, importing, finding bargains, coming up with thingamajigs that would make money. And it worked, particularly since he wasn't afraid of anything and he had guts. He had one sentence that he repeated often, "As long as you do something, anything can happen." And, miraculously, everything did happen. Money bred money.

But hanging in there, making progress, staying put, that wasn't for him. When things were working out and everything was going well, he began to get fed up. He would pack up and go, but not before he had destroyed everything he had built. Whether it was a restaurant in Mexico, a window washing company in downtown Montreal, an import-expert business in Park Extension, or a massage parlour. You name it.

When he was on the verge of an explosion, either psychological or physical, he would squander money, which seemed to burn a hole in his pocket. He would literally throw it out the window. A thousand dollars or ten thousand in small denominations would flutter in the air until it landed on the sidewalk, and he would be as happy as a child flying a kite.

He would then escape to the woods or to a fleabag hotel.

His ability to launch incredible businesses, which never failed to generate huge profits, was just as strong as his urge for destruction. And just as soon as a business began to prosper, he would make a point of undermining it, sabotaging everything, bringing it all down for fun, just for fun. It was as if he liked to build things up just for the pleasure of knocking them down again.

He didn't care about anything or anyone. Life itself was of little importance to him. To live or die – it was all the same to him.

He was well aware that if he did not control himself, he could wind up in prison. The frantic control of his violence stemmed from his all-consuming fear of imprisonment. This was the only situation he hated, the only place he abhorred after having had a taste of it for fourteen days and thirteen nights. He was too attached to action, independence, freedom, nature, although he was terrified by promiscuity. To be confined would be worse than death, especially if it hadn't been his choice.

He liked to be alone. For hours and sometimes days. When he was alone, he didn't have to try so hard to keep from hitting, breaking and destroying. When he was alone, he would sometimes punch the wall very hard. He would make his knuckles bleed. He was not averse to seeing blood, to feeling his skin burn. At least it was his own blood and he hadn't harmed anyone, in this Hutchison Street basement where he had been living for just a short while.

He could trash a luxury apartment just as easily as a miserable one-room flat, and then put everything back together again, or pay for the damage and then move. On very rare occasions, he had left without paying. When that happened, the landlord would get a cheque a few months or a few years later. Without a covering letter, without an apology. Words, whether they were written or spoken, were not his forte. His way of being and operating was nonverbal.

He was over forty and he had lived several lives. Lives without a past and without a future. He had not yet found his destination, and wasn't looking for one either. He had always lived his life this way and he didn't even know that it was possible to live any other way.

He had no strong ties to anyone. He wasn't attached to anyone – no family, no social, cultural, patriotic, religious affiliations. He spoke French, English, Spanish and Italian fairly well, without preference for any language. Even the phonetics professor Henry Higgins would not have been able to detect where he came from and where he had lived, since his accent – or rather accents – were vague and impenetrable. He had changed his name to Kowalski because he hated his father, and didn't want to hang on to anything that reminded him of his father. He chose Kowalski because he liked Stanley Kowalski, a character played by Marlon Brando in *A Streetcar Named Desire*. He had kept his given name, Ronald, but everyone he ran into called him Ron. He liked the name a lot, because it sounded like "run," like the title of the cult film, *Run Lola Run*, which he had seen a dozen times.

Here today, gone tomorrow. His only fixed address was a storage locker of a few cubic metres, which he had rented for ten years and paid for in a god-forsaken corner of Saint-Léonard.

He didn't know where he belonged, but he really didn't give a damn. One of a kind, not part of any gang, even when he was a teenager. He didn't conform to anything. He followed his own rules and his own laws. That made him feel superior to many other people he met.

Among other people, he seemed self-sufficient, sure

of himself. Alone with himself, he felt diminished by his rage and violence, which he would always have to keep on a tight leash, holding back and controlling himself.

His rage owned him: it kept him, he kept it at bay.

His body, his head, his feelings were never at rest, except when he was in the wilds, or when he was listening to a story. His love of stories dated back to when he was a little boy and his aunt, his mother's sister, used to come into his bedroom, bringing a new book each time. She would show him the pictures, one at a time, taking all the time in the world, and then tell him to lie down and close his eyes. She would then read the story from beginning to end. And he would fall asleep happy.

When he felt the need to hear a story, he would turn on the TV. But he was quickly disappointed, so he would switch off the television and rush off to the movies.

FRANÇOISE CAMIRAND

She had just bumped into Ron Kowalski. The one she had nicknamed "the free electron" had become just that, at his own expense. He would detach himself, he would split in two. She couldn't figure him out. First of all, she had pictured him clearly, but then, as she was writing about him, other people she had known in the past became superimposed on him and cluttered up the path she had taken.

There were more and more people like Ron Kowalski in Montreal and everywhere in the world. Young and old. Migrants, here and elsewhere, born in Poland, Italy, Israel, or in Montreal, Saint-Léonard or Baie-Comeau. It didn't matter where, these people are from nowhere.

A person can be a composite, but how could she make him into a unified person, someone like him who was fundamentally ineffable?

She had seen him several times, sometimes years apart. She had not forgotten him, but who could forget him? Then, recently, she saw him twice on Hutchison Street and once at the corner grocery store. He had almost not aged, he looked good and had a certain charisma. He had a good quality leather bag on his shoulder, he was well dressed and he carried himself well, but he couldn't stand still. He shifted from foot to foot, and looked ready to move right or left or straight ahead, it didn't matter, he just looked ready to pounce.

Ron Kowalski is the kind of person who in real life already looks like a fictional character. Whenever he walks into a place, people notice him. With sweeping gestures, a smirk on his face, he goes from one language to another with no hesitation and with no accent that reveals where he comes from. When he's standing up, he looks alert, when he's sitting down, he's always slouching and when he's smiling, it's to charm us to death. The only time you see the child in him is when he's laughing.

Françoise saw him burst out laughing in the grocery store when the oranges started to roll off the display case. No one was able to keep the oranges from falling off the shelf, not even him. When she heard him laugh like a bird cooing and saw him with his arms outstretched, she knew that he would become a character in her novel.

What enchanted her as much as his smile was the bond that formed immediately between Ron Kowalski and Jeannot Paterson, the store's lowly employee. All of a sudden, they started up a conversation with each other. Which was surprising, to say the least, since Jeannot Paterson was not making the inarticulate sounds he usually did. He was actually talking. He switched from English to French, just like Ron. It was the very first time that Françoise heard Jeannot's voice, and it occurred to her that Ron Kowalski must be a magician as well as a free electron.

JEANNOT PATERSON

His life didn't amount to much. For those who couldn't tell him apart from the counters at the grocery store where he worked, his life did not amount to much.

He could have been born a Gemini, Taurus, Libra or Capricorn, he was born under the sign of Fear. From early childhood – and perhaps even in his mother's womb – between a father who always had a beer in his hand and a mother who was prey to anxiety and panic attacks, he had caught a fear the way a child catches a cold, the flu or measles, without ever getting better. This fear had never left him, had never let him relax, had stuck to his skin, had hollowed out his belly, had made all of his limbs tremble, had carved lines in his face. His face had aged, he was drawn, and he was never calm. He never looked comfortable and self-assured, except perhaps when the door to the grocery store was double bolted and he had all the time in the world to wash the floor with a large mop soaked with plenty of soapy water.

His life didn't matter to anyone, but it was his life and he liked it. He had grown used to it. He had internalized his fear, he had learned to live with it, he could not have lived

194

without it, since it was so much a part of his personality.

He was called Jean Paterson, officially, on his health-care card, which he always carried on him, right next to the photo of his mother who had been dead for many years. When he was young, his mother called him Jeannot. On the rare occasion when his father talked to him, he called him John. At the grocery store, he was Johnny. When he talked to himself, to alleviate his fear, he would say: "You can do it, Jeannot, my boy, you know that you can." When he was angry with himself, when he couldn't go on any longer because he was paralyzed by fear, he would use his English name, repeating: "Come on, John, come on, John." It helped him. It helped him cross the street and deal with his problems. It helped him when he had to run to the basement or reach to the end of the counter to get something that someone had asked him for, "no, not the right-hand counter, Johnny, left, at your left-hand, Johnny, left, your left-hand, in front of you, down there, yes, down there to the left."

"You can do it, Jeannot, my boy, you know that you can." It helped him answer a customer who had noticed him and said hello to him. He would reply with a smile that looked like it had jumped out of an old jack-in-the-box. It was the dazzling smile of a child who had grown old by accident; it was a ray of sunshine that had nothing to do with the rest of him. Anyone who had seen him smile once would never forget it.

He didn't get many smiles or hellos. That didn't bother him. In fact, he liked it better if no one noticed him, if he was forgotten. *Bonjour*, *allô*, hello, hi, he would reply, if he had to, with an accent that was not identifiable, an accent that came from nowhere, just like his face and body, which looked like they were apologizing for existing.

How had Jeannot ended up on Hutchison Street when he was born and raised in Verdun and lived in constant fear? It was thanks to his friend Paul, his one and only friend. Paul had brought him to Outremont, almost holding his hand to get him there. They had taken a bus, then the metro, and then another bus, it was not easy to remember it all. His friend Paul had a neighbour, Jorge Mihelakis, who had an uncle who had a grocery store at the corner of Bernard and Hutchison, and the uncle was in need of a helper. Someone who would keep the store clean. Jeannot was the ideal person for this kind of work. Jorge's uncle found the perfect helper, who never said a word louder than anyone else, who never said a word period, even though he knew how to talk, who did everything he was asked to do right away without grumbling or grousing, without saying, "But I just did that!" Mr. Mihelakis wanted to hang on to his helper, and needed him to be close at hand, so he found him a room a couple of doors down from the store.

When you saw Jeannot, Jean, John, or Johnny carefully sweeping or washing the floors between the aisles in the grocery store, you would never know that Jeannot often had a stomach ache because he was afraid. That was because Jeannot was not afraid when he was doing repetitive chores. Day after day, the repetitive movements were like caresses. If Mr. Mihelakis shouted "Johnny" from one end of the store to the other, if he was in a hurry and Johnny had to do something quickly, he would once again be overcome by fear. Johnny would come running, muttering, "come on, John, come on, John," but he was afraid, so afraid that his heart raced and his stomach hurt. And yet, Mr. Mihelakis had never hit him. Never.

Mr. Mihelakis was very kind to him. Johnny could eat all he wanted in the store and drink as much as he liked, anything except beer or wine. He could even go outside to smoke. Summer and winter, the moments he spent smoking alone outside made him totally happy. You burn through one cigarette very quickly and his boss was very clear about that – only one cigarette at a time. There was no lunch hour or dinner hour, not even a half hour, although Johnny could eat any time. Mr. Mihelakis didn't take a break for meals either. They each ate whenever they were hungry, or whenever they could, taking advantage of a quiet moment, but as all small shopkeepers will tell you, it's always just as you're taking your first bite that someone will come in to bother you. Everyone knows that. Mr. Mihelakis and Johnny knew it better than anyone and they never complained.

Several times a day, Johnny went to get two large cups of coffee, one for him and one for Mr. Mihelakis, at the Buy More restaurant across the street. When Buy More closed down, Mr. Mihelakis bought an electric coffee maker. It was Johnny's job to make a good pot of coffee, and Mr. Mihelakis was very happy. Johnny liked good coffee and liked it when Mr. Mihelakis was happy. He often went out to smoke a cigarette with a coffee in his hand. Even when it was cold out, he would go out with his parka open and his bare neck exposed to the elements, feeling like a king standing outside surveying his kingdom.

Around nine o'clock in the evening, Mr. Mihelakis would lock the door and do the cash. He would put an envelope in his pocket and go put the money in the night deposit at the TD Bank just across the street. That's when Johnny had the grocery store all to himself. Mr. Mihelakis trusted him and Johnny was proud of that. He could take his time cleaning up, putting things away, and drinking a little apple juice without any interruptions. He could even munch on a chocolate bar, or empty a bag of chips if he wanted, and then turn off the lights, lock the door, check to see that the locks were secure, and slowly walk back to his room in the basement of a beautiful house on Hutchison Street, just two minutes from the store. He would sleep a bit, then wake up to start another great day.

His only dream was to become so used to his work that he would never again make any mistakes. He was making fewer and fewer, but he was so unhappy if it ever happened. Jeannot loved his work. Johnny loved Mr. Mihelakis and Mr. Mihelakis loved him. There was no way that Jeannot Paterson wanted to be sent back to his father in Verdun.

THE DIARY OF HINDA ROCHEL

Phew! I have time to write. The other day a woman who was almost as old as Madame Genest came up to talk to me. I have seen her often. She lives just across the street from us. She stopped me in the street and spoke to me in French. I write and read French, but when I have to speak it, I get very nervous, and I stutter a bit. I don't often get a chance to speak. I do with Madame Genest in school. I speak English or Yiddish with my friends, and we speak mainly English when we are together. The woman had a piece of paper in her hand with columns full of Jewish names, first names and family names. She asked me if the names were Hasidic. I was surprised. This was the first time that someone has stopped me in the street to ask me a question. People know who we are and they don't bother us. They avoid looking at us, they walk past as if we don't exist. Except sometimes. I have seen mean people staring at us, but not very often. Sometimes, they look like they feel sorry for us. I see people talking to one another as they come toward us, they're looking at us from a distance and I know they are talking about us. From the look on their faces, I can see that they are wondering how we can live like this, especially in summer when it's very hot out, and for us it makes no difference whether it's hot. It's just like me, when I see my neighbours I wonder how they can walk down the street showing their legs, their thighs and their breasts as if they were at the *mikvah* with no one else around.

I'm writing and writing, and I have forgotten that I wanted to talk about that lady. I'm happy today. I'm all alone in the house and I have the time to write as much as I like. I'm sick, that's why. The whole family has gone to spend Shabbat with my grandmother. "Rest," my mother said. It's because it's Shabbat that she said that, not because I'm sick. You have to rest on Shabbat. I don't know if it's forbidden to write. My mother has never said so. So I'm just doing it. For me, writing is resting.

I have seen that woman often. In summer, she is always dressed in white. In winter in black. I have already seen her smile at the little kids in our community, but never to girls my age or to the grown-ups. Before she spoke to me, she smiled. I was very close to home. I saw her cross the street and come up to me. Her smile surprised me very much. I didn't smile back. But when I saw all those Jewish names on her piece of paper, I smiled. There were three columns, printed out by computer, a column for boys' names, one for girls' names, and another for family names. She had a pen in her hand and she gave it to me so that I could check off the Hasidic names. I checked all the names I knew beginning with the names of my brothers, sisters, cousins and friends. My name was not in her columns but I didn't tell her. She said thank you and pointed at my house. "You live there, don't you?" I said yes. She waved to me and was about to cross the street, when I asked her, "Do you like Gabrielle Roy?" I don't know why I did that, the words just

200

popped out of my mouth. She turned to me with a smile and a surprised look on her face, "Of course, and you? Do you know who Gabrielle Roy is?" I answered, "Yes and I like her a lot." She had such a smile on her face, and she looked like she couldn't believe what she was hearing. Then she asked, "What have you read by her?" I said, "The only book I've read is *Bonheur d'occasion*." "And did you like it?" "I've read it thirteen times." I added one time without realizing it. My mother always says that I should be careful. Lying is covered by the 613 *mizvot*. Many other things, too, but it's too long to write about. My mother often says that I exaggerate, and that exaggerating is close to lying and that it's bad. For my mother, everything is bad.

The woman was already on the other side of the street about to walk up the stairs of her building when I saw her turn around and head back over toward me. She waited for the cars to go past and then crossed the street. She asked me, "And you, is your name on my list, what's your name?" I said, "No. My name is Hinda Rochel." She said, "Hinda is a pretty name." I said, "No, Hinda Rochel. That's me. The family name is Hertog." "You have a double name, that's unusual, isn't it?" "Yes, it's rare," I replied. She smiled and said, *mazel tov*. She waved again and crossed the street. I was left with her *mazel tov*. You say *mazel tov* when someone gets married, when a baby is born, when someone buys a house or a car, but not for a name, even a double one. For her, it was perhaps a very special occasion to speak to a Hasidic girl. It was for me, too. Apart from my French teachers, I have never told anyone my name. I mean, I haven't told a stranger. No one has ever asked.

ALBERT DUPRAS

Just as he was opening his eyes, one morning in May, he heard them talking about him on the radio. Anyone else would have had shivers down his spine hearing his name in the same breath as the words liar, cruel, pitbull, disgusting, petty, asshole, monster or rat. One of those labels alone would have been enough to upset anyone. But not him. It wasn't the first time this had happened, and he had long since steeled himself for this kind of abuse. Groggy as he was, he was smiling. If they were saying bad things about him, it was because he had done his job. Two things counted for him: doing his job well and getting people to talk about him. The more he was despised, the better known he was, and the better known he was, the farther he could afford to go. He had achieved what he had set out to do.

Each time they mentioned his name in the media, backstage, or in conversations among connoisseurs, he could take revenge for his wasted childhood and his miserable youth.

When he was young, he was the ugliest, the shortest, the fattest. The loneliest. He was also the bravest.

How many times had he found himself without a coat, without shoes, with a bloody nose? How many times had the others humiliated him, poked fun at him, ridiculed him, ostracized him, or looked down at him with disgust as if he were nothing more than a dog turd? He could hardly wait until he was eighteen years old so that he could escape from his lousy home town, where he felt so alone, so alienated from everyone else. Despite all the hardship and distress he had felt since his first day at school, despite the dread he felt every minute of the day with no one to talk about it, little Albert had never missed a day of school. Never. Even though leaving home, walking three blocks, slinking along the walls and slipping into the classroom was like swimming across an icy lake, one hundred and eighty days of the year, for eleven years. Still, he never missed a day. He had boundless courage, without question, and intelligence, to boot.

He had read everything and he could make verbal mincemeat out of any smarty-pants, teachers included, who came along. A walking encyclopedia, he would mesmerize them with his vast knowledge of everything, although that wouldn't prevent the stupid louts from treating him like a fairy for the same reasons.

But he knew that the long hours he spent reading alone, which gave him a lot of pleasure, would one day do more for him that just that. They would pay off. Oh, yes, they would pay off! Those who were laughing today, who had been humiliating him since he was a child, would very soon be "eating their own shit," as he saw it.

"One day you'll see, you'll see, *mes tabarnaks* …" How many times had he chanted this mantra to himself, how many times had he repeated the words with those very guys in mind, the ones who had pissed him off and made fun of him, who had looked down their nose at him or scorned him. His outbursts were peppered with *tabernacles*, *hosties*, *ciboires* and *calices*. Although his vocabulary was rich enough to keep up with hip hop artists like Loco Locass, he preferred to use the religious swearwords of Quebec, which was the only way he knew to express his rage fully and find a bit of relief from the dumb thugs who humiliated him relentlessly.

When he was young, he didn't know how to enjoy the insults yet. First, he had to be successful. And he swore that he would succeed. That he would triumph, even.

This morning, while listening to the excited boor on the radio, Albert wasn't swearing. It was a treat. When people said or wrote bad things about him, or sent him insulting letters, packages of shit, he was ecstatic. He revelled in the violent harangue, the low-class outpouring, the unimpressive settling of scores, and hoped that it would go on forever. It was music to his ears, like Glenn Gould playing Bach fugues … He smiled. He stretched his limbs as he lay in bed, happy.

You could say that there was nothing attractive about Albert's face, except his smile, which few people had seen. His smile was possibly the only thing he had hung on to from childhood, from the pre-school years when his mother found him beautiful. His smile was a tiny bit coy, a bit shy, a bit love-me-I-am-lovable-I-swear. Without the smile, he would have looked like a gnome. He had the outward appearance of a gnome, but, above all, he was shrewd and perceptive – defining qualities in those little deformed creatures that inhabit the interior of the Earth and guard its treasures ... or else transform them at will into their opposites.

When Albert Dupras began working as a journalist – before his success went to his head – everyone recognized his intelligence and vast general knowledge. He was one of those rare critics who could write a penetrating and sound analysis that would shed light on a particular work and put it into perspective. Whether you agreed with what he said or not, you had to hand it to him and admire his elegant style.

But in order to become well known and to ensure that people would go on talking about him, he had to go a bit further. He was intelligent enough to know that people often confuse being nice and being insipid, that being nice does not earn you respect, and that small people kowtow to those they fear. It was clear that to be successful, to shine, he had to be controversial. Now that he had proven that he was good, very good, he had to show that he was the best, indisputably, like the French critics he adored, whom he read diligently and whom he wanted to imitate. So he had to start rocking the boat and shining the spot-light on himself.

He knew how to turn a phrase, and he wrote well, so

he was able to cut anyone down with just a few words. But what he did was more subtle and yielded greater dividends as far as getting attention was concerned. He would praise an artist to the hilt, portray him in superlatives worthy of a god, and then, after the next performance, with one swift blow, knock him off the pedestal on which he himself had placed him. Without any artistic justification. It surprised people and got them talking. "He's probably right," they would say. "Oh, do you think so?" "Well, come on, he knows what he's talking about, he's the best!"

At the beginning, he was just testing the waters. He didn't know that it would work out so well. When he said that someone or another was a genius, he actually meant it, and when he pulled the rug out from under their feet after the next show, he had his reasons. Perhaps the performer in question hadn't smiled at him, or else hadn't said thank you. Or was it just to have a bit of fun? For the pleasure of seeing panic in the eyes of the people he ran across. For the sense of power it gave him. Which he began to love, quite a lot, deeply.

He got tougher. He began to attack artists personally and dig into their personal lives. With a well-turned phrase, sometimes with sexual overtones. Of course, he was very gentle, at the beginning. But he saw that his tactics were beginning to pay off. People were talking about him. More and more. Oh, the happiness.

Gradually, the two things that mattered the most to him – doing a good job and making sure people were talking about him – got switched around. It became more important, far more important, for people to talk about him. He was on the verge of becoming a celebrity.

"One day you'll see, *mes tabarnaks*." They say that revenge is a dish that's best served cold, but revenge also has a way of whetting your appetite. He was never satisfied.

People were afraid of him and people hated him. Nevertheless, they read what he wrote, they responded to his articles. He had become THE authority, now that he had power. Power, or rather a feeling of power, is like a hard drug, just as bad as heroin. Although heroin is widely decried, once you have experienced its power, you give in. Once you get a taste of it, it is hard to do without, especially if the substance gives you what you have been seeking for a long time. Controlling the fate of other people can be a source of incredible pleasure. Seeing the impact of a few words you have written can give you such a kick, such a high. Especially seeing fear in the eyes of artists. Yes, just seeing fear in other people can be such a thrill.

The power he had in his circle was so great that even he could not believe the devastation he caused. Highly talented artists were defeated, crushed, reduced to tears. Critics writing for other papers were no longer important. People read them but didn't really pay much attention to what they were saying. There was only one legitimate opinion, like the sacred message propagated by a single evangelist, the gospel according to Albert Dupras. His reviews – both good and bad – wreaked havoc because people believed what he said. And so did he. He had fallen into his own trap.

The day when no one wanted to have anything more to do with his power and he was forbidden from entering a theatre or concert hall, he felt as if he had hit the jackpot. It was unhoped for. How could he, Quebec's greatest critic, be prevented from carrying out his duties? He was the victim now, a role that he was even more familiar with than the executioner's role. He wasn't going to let them get the best of him, oh no, you'll see, *mes tabarnaks*, you'll soon see my true colours, you haven't seen anything yet. He bought a ticket and went in. Incognito. He had always had courage to burn since he was a child and he had always been galvanized by adversity, as long as it wasn't physical.

A star was born, people were saying, using the English cliché. Albert Dupras was invited to speak on panels and was a guest on all the talk shows. He had become more famous than many of the entertainers he had either demolished or praised to the hilt – always one extreme or the other – to provoke indignation and stir things up, to generate controversy and hold people's attention.

It was glorious. Even more amazing than he could have dreamed of. The assholes who had tormented him back in Jonquière didn't read the papers, for sure, but they would have seen him on television, *les calices*. He was anxious to go back home to see his mother, if only to see the look on the stupid, uneducated faces of those morons.

He waits for the interview to end and then gets up, humming a tune. There's no one with him this morning. He came home alone last night. He's been afraid since he was beat up and mugged by a young hoodlum. No matter how much he delights in verbal violence, he dreads physical violence. He has been terrorized since the age of six, when he was knocked down on an icy sidewalk, held down by two strong arms, with legs all around him, and snow in his eyes, in his ears and down his neck. He completely loses control at the least sign of aggression. He sometimes wonders how he managed to get through his childhood and teenage years without dying. Without giving in to fear.

He makes a pot of coffee, drinks two cups one after the other, without eating. He puts on the first t-shirt he can lay his hands on, which is spread out on the back of a chair, and steps into a pair of beige shorts that he hasn't washed for a long time. He hurries out to pick up the papers at the corner store, as he does every morning.

He has been living on Hutchison Street for two years, but he hasn't met anyone he knows, except the actresses who live across the street. He thought it was best to leave them out of the picture. He runs down the stairs, turns left, and sees a man leaning against the wall of the TD Bank three doors up from his house. He recognizes him. "Oh my god, he knows where I live and has been waiting for me to go out." The man smiles at him. It was a smile that gave him goose bumps.

He quickly crosses the street so that he doesn't have to pass by the man, then he turns onto Bernard and goes over to Park Avenue. Once he's got the newspapers under his arm, instead of turning around and going directly home, he goes south on Park Avenue. He walks briskly, past the YMCA on the corner of Saint-Viateur. His heart is beating so fast that he fears his chest will explode. When he gets back to Hutchison he slows down. The man must still be there.

He had had so much fun denigrating this guy. He had talked about his pretty face rather than his acting ability. He had written that young Boissonneau would have been better off getting a job in a night club for single women, wiggling his pretty butt around all night, because that's all he knew how to do, instead of massacring Molière and insulting the audience's intelligence.

Had he gone too far? No. The guy was a bad actor. Albert Dupras knew that, more than anyone else. Albert Dupras was the best critic, and what he found bad was actually bad because he had seen it with his own eyes. He had thought it with his own brain, and had written it up in the newspaper.

"Perhaps I overdid it, perhaps I could have put it differently. But I was right. I know I was right. I am paid for that. To be right."

From a distance, he can see the actor in the same position, his back against the wall and his right leg crossed over his left leg. He hasn't budged an inch. "Oh my god, oh my god, oh my god!" Albert begins to shake uncontrollably.

It didn't occur to him, not for one second, that he could have taken the alleyway to sneak into his house through the back door …

XAROULA AND HER SISTERS

Even before Xaroula was born, the Koutsoukis family had a clan of girls and a clan of boys. The eldest and the second eldest girls already formed a solid duo when the three boys were born, close together. When Xaroula, the youngest, was born, her two big sisters took her under their wing. Not that the boys were mean to her, on the contrary, but that's the way it was, the girls stuck with the girls and the boys with the boys.

Over the years, the relations between the girls and boys stayed the same. The girls got along well with each other and each boy got along with the other boys. There were no quarrels between the clans, although they were not attached to one another either. You could say that there were two families in one.

The brothers and sisters did not see each other often. When their parents were still alive, the whole family got together a few times a year, for Christmas and New Year's and especially for Greek Orthodox Easter. Once their father died and then their mother, the two clans split further apart. The boys had attended their parents' funerals, but they had behaved like third cousins and hadn't lifted a finger to help with the arrangements for the service or reception. In any case, their two older sisters wouldn't have let them do anything. Each member of the family reverted to the role they had always assumed: the two older girls looked after everything and the youngest cried; the boys waited for it to be over, while drinking, eating and handing out their business cards. It's surprising how many people you see only at funerals.

The three-storey house had been bought by their father at the beginning of the 1970s. He had been a prosperous businessman and had worked tirelessly until the day he dropped dead, when his worn-out heart just stopped beating. Their mother passed away more recently. The Koutsoukis family lived on the ground floor and rented out the two upper floors to strangers – they referred to all those who were not Greek as strangers. The four youngest had been born in the house. Over the years, they had all left to get married, travel, escape from the grip of the family, and live their lives. Everyone except Xaroula, the youngest.

After CEGEP, Xaroula wasn't at all interested in going on to university, but she was even less tempted to go out to work. She had no girlfriends and no boyfriend, she didn't go out, she never went to the movies or anywhere else. For unknown reasons, she didn't aspire to get married, have children, or anything else. She had kept the room she had as a schoolgirl and the habits that went along with it. She was willing to go out to get the groceries once a week and she would do one or two errands at the corner grocery store, without having her arm twisted to do so. Other than that, she would spend her days sitting in the big stuffed chair on the front balcony when the weather was nice, with earphones on her head, and in her bedroom for the rest of the year, listening to Greek songs.

Greek music was the one and only thing that made her feel alive. And yet, Xaroula wasn't born in Greece, she hadn't lived there, except for three weeks at the age of twenty when her father treated her to a trip over there, and she had come back with a suitcase packed full of music, which she had been listening to every since.

Her mother was not unhappy to have her stay home and keep her company. Even though her daughter didn't help out very much, she felt less lonely after her children had left home and her husband had died. Xaroula's sisters, on the other hand, were stunned to see her vegetate and didn't know what more they could do to get Xaroula to move her ass. "If you don't want to work or study, at least go out and find yourself a husband." Her behaviour, her complete lack of motivation, was totally unlike any of the other family members, who had made their way in life, each in their own way.

When her mother got sick, two years before she died, Xaroula changed completely. She became a responsible young woman and looked after her very well. Her sisters were very relieved and never talked to her again about finding a husband or a job.

When their mother died, the family house, the three apartment buildings in Park Extension, and money that their father had saved, was divided up equally among the six children. The three boys gave their share of the inheritance to Xaroula. They had enough money, thank God, and the apartment buildings that their father had picked up for a song only gave them headaches and generated little profit. As for the family house, they said that Xaroula was comfortable where she was and that with the rent from the tenants she would have a decent income.

This arrangement, agreed upon in less than five minutes, was perfectly fine with the girls.

Xaroula then found herself alone in a big apartment. Because her mother had occupied an important place in her life for the past two years, she was distraught and cried all day. She couldn't even listen to her beloved Greek music anymore. She felt old, very old. She didn't have a mom anymore, or a dad. All of her life felt like a long colourless and monotonous chain leading up to death.

Her older sister, Adhriani, was also going through hard times. She had sold her shares in the import-export company she had started up with her husband. She had just gotten divorced, and her two children, who were old enough to choose, had decided to go live with their father because they felt like their mother always wanted to control everything. Adhriani knew she was no angel, she knew she was authoritarian, but she felt that being stabbed in the back by the children she loved so much was more than she deserved. Her husband kept the house because of the kids, and she found herself in a nowhere-to-go situation, which made her head spin and gave her a funny feeling she had never had, not even when she had gotten off the boat with her parents in this new country at the age of six.

Eliana, the second child, was no better off than the eldest. She had ditched her boyfriend because he didn't want kids and because for her it was now or never. Her downtown shop had been limping along for the past few years, and she was fed up with the retail business. She wanted to change course, sell the business, stop, catch her breath and think about the future. Maybe start something with Adhriani, "a shop, an agency, a restaurant, something new, for God's sake." Perhaps go back to sculpture again, it had been her passion when she was younger, "why not, better late than never."

And so it happened that the members of the girls' clan were reunited in the family house again, shortly after the death of their mother.

It's a beautiful day in May and the three sisters are sitting out on the balcony in comfortable upholstered chairs. One is reading a novel, the other is leafing through a magazine and the third is listening to music. They look calm. Adhriani places her book on her lap and looks out at Hutchison Street, which hasn't changed a lot since she used to skip rope with Eliana. The sidewalk on the Mile End side has been widened and the trees have grown taller, that's all. A Hasidic family is walking at a good clip toward Saint-Viateur. On the Outremont side of the street, just in front of her, an old lady is moving slowly, leaning on her walker for support. Adhriani watches her for a long time until she gets up to the TD Bank at the corner of Bernard and disappears from view. Adhriani looks at her sisters and ponders for a moment. Then she looks straight ahead, glances back again at her sisters, and bursts out laughing.

She says to them in Greek, "Eliana and I have worked our tootsies off, going flat out to carve out a place for ourselves and make a bit of money. And for what? To come back to exactly the same place, the same balcony, to watch life go by before our very eyes as if we had never left. Xaroula was right all along." And she laughs ... "Don't you think, my dear sisters, that we are like the Three Graces? Beauty, art, fertility – the Three Graces from Greek mythology, that's us. Xaroula is beauty, Eliana is art, and I am fertility. My children don't want to see me anymore, but that doesn't change anything, they still came from my womb!" And she laughs.

Taken aback by their sister's merriment, Xaroula and Eliana begin to laugh too. To keep her company. Sometimes, laughing alone is more painful than crying.

THE DIARY OF HINDA ROCHEL

Today, I got a big surprise. There was a white plastic bag hanging from the doorknob of our house. I thought it was the bag that comes full of advertising. I looked inside before going to throw it into the recycling bin. It was a book. *Ces enfants de ma vie*. With a little boy drawn by hand on the front cover and a photo of Gabrielle Roy on the back. I have never seen Gabrielle Roy because on my copy of *Bonheur d'occasion*, which I found on the sidewalk two years ago now, there is no photo. In the bag, there was also a card with handwriting on it. I quickly opened my school bag and stuffed it all inside before my mother could ask me what it was. I could hear her coming with my little brother in her arms. I pretended that I had to go very badly and then I ran into the bathroom. I was safe in there, I could look at my book for as long as I wanted until someone made me get out of the bathroom. Gabrielle Roy has a pretty face, but she is old. She looks like my grandmother except with real hair. I thought she would be as young as her character Florentine. On the card, it said, "I have as many books as you like. Come knock on the door. I live right across the street. Enjoy the book! Françoise Camirand."

I only had time to read the first sentence of the book, which

217

I already know by heart: "When I think back, as I often do these days, to my years as a young teacher in a city school for boys, the first picture that comes, emotion-charged as ever, is that of the opening morning."[7]

Gabrielle Roy uses a lot of commas. I don't ever know where to put commas. Sometimes I don't even know where to put periods.

FRANÇOISE CAMIRAND

When she began to write this book, she had a feeling that nothing would ever be the same. She was taking a new turn, going down a new road. The farther she got, the more the road widened. "It's not a joke, she said to herself, but my beautiful Hutchison Street has become a BOULEVARD!" Even if she worked on it for twenty years, she would not run out of material. Her street was teeming with characters. She had already selected more than twenty.

In her dreams, she sometimes saw them coming up to her, arm in arm, walking in step, a real little army. Even those she had dropped in the course of writing the book were in the ranks.

Around twenty short novels, lives that were awaiting the eyes of the reader or the passerby.

She now knew the real name of the little Jewish girl she had seen in a dream. Her smile was even more beautiful in real life, and her cheeks had become all red when she, Hinda Rochel, had talked about Gabrielle Roy. Françoise had been so surprised that she had also blushed. She was still flabbergasted when she got home. Who would have thought that a young Hasidic girl could have read *Bonheur d'occasion* thirteen times, certainly not Françoise. Until then, she was practically certain that the Hasidim did not speak French. She thought that Hinda Rochel was surely the exception that proved the rule. Perhaps she was wrong, and there were more than she thought, she had just never heard them.

In any case, it was the first time in thirty-nine years that she was reaching out to them, that she was testing the waters, so to speak.

WILLA COLERIDGE

She had walked past the synagogue at the corner of her street hundreds of times, if not thousands. She had had the urge to go in hundreds of times, but had never had the courage to try it. Men were going in through the main entrance on Hutchison Street and the women were using the side door on Saint-Viateur. It would have been a sacrilege to go in through the men's door, even daring to think about it. But the women's entrance, in her head at least, was doable. Except that she lost her nerve every time. She asked herself, "What would be the worst thing that could happen to me? That they would forbid me to go in? That they would throw me out forcibly? Well, I would just go back out, that's all. What's preventing me from trying? I should try it, at least." Standing in front of the forbidden door, the same thoughts would swirl around in her head each time. They would heat up her body and slow down her step, and she would walk on by. She was annoyed with herself. "These people are peaceful, they won't hurt me, so why am I so afraid?"

It was Saturday. A glorious day when the heat, light and

gentle breeze seemed to conspire to fill her with joy. That's why the residents of Hutchison Street liked to say that rather than have a rainy, blistering hot or muggy June-July-August, it would be better for the month of May to last all summer.

Willa Coleridge went out onto her balcony with a steaming cup of coffee in her hand. Standing there, with her back leaning up against the brick wall, she sniffed the air before sitting down at her old coffee table with the paint chipped off. She dropped three sugar cubes into the cup, stirred the coffee carefully, and sipped it. The coffee was good. Another beautiful day had begun. On the other side of the street she could see Xaroula Koutsoukis turned sideways, with her legs outstretched and a large set of earphones perched on her head, and Albert Dupras who was running down the stairs in the pair of khaki Bermuda shorts he always wore. At this very instant, she could have photographed them as she had so often done in her imagination, without being able to attach a name to the faces in her make-believe photo. She had seen them so often, the woman sitting in her stuffed chair that looked so comfy and the man running up or down his stairs carrying a case of beer or an armload of newspapers. She had bumped into them so often, she had smiled at them – a smile of recognition, between neighbours. Xaroula, with her earphones and iPod, would smile shyly, while Albert, always in a hurry, always engrossed in thought, didn't see her smile and therefore didn't respond to it.

Albert Dupras was coming home, almost running.

He ran up the stairs with a pile of papers and magazines. Willa smiled and wondered what the guy across the street could possibly be doing with all those newspapers. He would read them, of course, but she had the impression that this man, who was always carrying either newspapers or bottles of beer, was particularly attached to those two things. He was always in a hurry, like the Hasidim, but he looked more nervous than they did. When she came home from work, late at night, she would see him out on his balcony, subdued for a change, immersed in his reading, with a beer in his hand. He didn't have a wife, or children either, she was sure of that, she would have noticed if he did.

She went back inside to pour herself another cup of coffee and then went out again. Almost deserted a short while ago, the street was lively now. Watching people while drinking her coffee, especially when the weather was nice, was Willa's entertainment. It fulfilled a need, it gave her pleasure, even more than any television program would.

Men with their sons, women with their daughters, walked southward on both sides of the street. The men were wearing black satin suits, white stockings, and some had wide fur hats on. They were all clean and dressed up. "It's Saturday, and the Hasidim are going to mass," she thought. She knew that it was their Sabbath, that they were all going off to pray and chant, and that her neighbours prayed often and a lot. Shabbat was their Sunday, she knew that much, but she didn't know what they called the service they held on Saturday, which was their holy day.

She certainly wanted to get to know them and to learn more about them, there was no doubt about that. But how? So far, all her attempts had fallen flat. Not even a smile of recognition among neighbours. Never. One solution would have been to read up on them, but reading wasn't her thing. Willa was more down-to-earth, she liked direct contact, she liked to get to know people and to hear them tell their stories face to face. She liked to touch people with her hands and see things with her own eyes, for real.

She got up and leaned on the balcony railing. She watched the flow of human beings down below as they moved along, soundlessly, all going to the same place with a sense of determination and fulfilment. She was envious. She, too, would have liked to belong to a community. Of course, she had her church, which she attended every Sunday. For the Hasidim, though, every day was like one of her Sundays. They supported one another, they had the same God, they observed the same rules and they said the same prayers. They celebrated the same holidays and chanted the same melodies. Their lives were all planned out in advance. Shoulder to shoulder. This is the way life is, until death, each person bolstered by the others, and each person supporting the other members of the group. For them, there was no such thing as anxiety. Naturally, there's no anxiety when you know where you're going and how to get there. Life and death were simple and beautiful. The way is paved, clearly marked with milestones along the way. All you have to do is follow the path. Everything is prearranged so that you don't have to ask yourself any questions. You do what you have to do, and that's it. Willa was tired of asking questions and getting answers that changed all the time. How was she supposed to keep her spirits up when she was just treading water, day after day, without help or support, with no real ties to anyone, no one to take her hand and show her the way?

She thought about her own life as she continued to watch this river of humanity. The coffee spoon that she was holding slipped out of her hand and dropped onto the sidewalk beside a twelve-year-old girl. The girl looked up. Willa smiled at her to indicate that she was the one who had accidentally dropped the spoon. The girl smiled back at her. A lovely smile. My God. A big girl had smiled at her. My God. Not a baby. A girl who was almost an adult, who would get married in a few years.

This was the first time in twenty-five years that a Jewish person had smiled at her.

For Willa, this was a sign. The girl, who was walking along with her mother, was already way down the street, but something was stirring in Willa's heart.

The sidewalks became empty again. Willa went back inside treasuring the long-awaited smile. Her children would still be asleep. Friday was their night out and none of them would wake up until one o'clock in the afternoon on a Saturday. She put her jacket on, grabbed her bag and went out. She picked up the spoon she had dropped, stuffed it into her purse, and walked in the direction of Saint-Viateur.

She walked past the men's entrance and kept on going until she reached the women's entrance. You needed to have a code to get in, she knew that. She waited, her heart beating. A woman was coming around the YMCA building, stepping along in a hurry. Willa knew where she was going and adjusted her steps so that she would arrive at the entrance at the same time as her. The woman punched the code in quickly and opened the door. Without a moment's hesitation, Willa slipped in behind the woman and followed her through the open door. The woman stopped, baffled. Not knowing what to do with this voluptuous black woman who greeted her politely and said *Shalom* to her, she let her in. The woman knew all the people who attended their synagogue, and there were no blacks in the community, but what else could she do? Stop her from coming in? Get into a fight with her? She was already late.

The woman quickly walked down the long hallway without looking back, hoping that no one would see her arriving with this Goy, and a black one to boot. Willa had to walk twice as fast to keep up with her. The service had already begun. She could hear the men chanting. At the end of the hall, they went up a few stairs and Willa found herself in the women's gallery, just like in her dreams. It looked like her balcony, only three times as big, with a wooden railing and curtains that had been drawn open. There were a few rows of women, young and old, sitting on straight-backed chairs. Down below, the men were standing, crowded together, wearing prayer shawls, which she had caught a glimpse of before. Willa sat down, off to the side. Two women were whispering to one another. Two others were giggling. No one had noticed that she was there. A man standing at a small pulpit was singing by himself. Willa was stunned. What was she doing here? Then the man at the pulpit began to talk and the men answered "Amen," which was the only word she understood. Willa felt as if she were in a dream. Where on earth did she get this desire to make friends with these people? She was so afraid that someone would notice her that she didn't dare to breathe or move. She was an intruder, that's what she was, she had forced her way into a place where she was not wanted.

Seated right next to the door, she could have left without making a sound. Out of sight, out of mind. But, inexplicably, something deep down held her there. "What has come over me, what has come over me? Am I crazy or what?" She wanted to see it with her very own eyes, that's what she had wanted. But she was no further ahead. The mystery of the Hasidic Jews of Hutchison Street was unfathomable. What had she expected to achieve by coming here? To eliminate the barriers? To understand. But understand what? To belong to a community with closed doors?

The prayers started up again, then the chanting, but she didn't hear any of the women chanting or praying.

Perhaps they prayed inwardly. She spotted the girl who had smiled at her a little earlier. When the girl turned around and saw her, she looked terrified and blushed deeply. She looked the other way and bowed her head, slouching down in her chair as if she wanted to disappear.

Suddenly, Willa felt like a Black person. Not a non-Jew surrounded by Jews. But a Black woman in a world of Whites.

Black. Out of place.

The uneasiness of the young Jewish girl had reminded her of her own childhood. When she was a child or teenager, at times when she least expected it, she too would feel uncomfortable. She would feel embarrassed about being who she was. It was a constant struggle. The struggle of someone who is never the same as other people, the struggle of someone who has to apologize for who she is, and the struggle of someone who always has to bear in mind, and never forget, that black is beautiful, too, to avoid falling prey to self-loathing. As her father used to remind her repeatedly, "Don't you ever forget, Willa. Black is beautiful."

She wanted to disappear.

The service was over. The women stood up and got ready to leave. Each one of them looked at her before leaving, except the woman who had let her in. They were whispering in the staircase and in the hallway. A chill came over Willa, who sat there, glued to her chair, unable to get up.

A mature-looking woman, no doubt the wife of the

rabbi or some other influential person in the community, went up to her and said, "*Shabbat Shalom*." Then, she continued in English, "You're not Jewish, are you?" Willa shook her head. "Why did you come?" asked the woman. "To pray with you," Willa mumbled.

"Well, come again, next Shabbat, if you like," the woman said, although Willa could tell from her face that she didn't mean it. And with a gesture that was quite explicit, she suggested that Willa leave.

Willa left the women's gallery, went down the stairs, walked the length of the corridor like a sleepwalker. Still in a daze, she walked along without seeing anything around her. Men were gathering on the sidewalk of Hutchison Street in front of the synagogue. Willa had to step off the curb to get around them.

Something suddenly occurred to her that made her smile. If someone had come to her place and said to her, a person who had been born Black, "I want to become Black," she would have laughed. That's for sure. If she asked the Jews their permission to be part of their community, they would burst out laughing. There's absolutely no doubt about it.

FRANÇOISE CAMIRAND

She had been working all day on Marie Lajoie, a new character, and no doubt the last one. The first time she saw her, Françoise had just moved in with her gang of friends. She was sixteen years old and, from her perspective as a young woman, Marie Lajoie already seemed like an old lady. At the time, she was about the age Françoise was now. It made Françoise smile to think about it.

The more she worked, the more she liked her, and she even hoped that she would be like her if she ever reached such a ripe old age. Marie Lajoie must have been beautiful when she was young. Françoise found her stunning at eighty-nine.

She had often seen her walking on the Outremont side of the street, at first without a cane. But about ten years ago, the cane appeared, and Marie Lajoie had never been seen without it since that time. She had always been tiny, but with the years, her body had become frail and her hair white, although her back had remained perfectly straight. Always elegant and well put together, she went out for a walk every day, even in winter as long as the sidewalks were not icy. She would sometimes stop to catch her breath, talk to a child, or narrowly avoid being knocked over by a scooter or a bicycle. Walking on Hutchison Street between Saint-Viateur and Bernard had become a tricky business, sometimes even risky.

Françoise had often seen her in the neighbourhood shops, or standing at her window, her hand resting against the windowpane, or sitting on her balcony with a small straw hat on her head. Now that she was writing about Marie Lajoie, she recalled bits of conversation they had had together in the grocery store, at the drugstore, or even on the street.

About a year ago, Marie Lajoie and Françoise had seen a piano and its owner moving in, just across from Marie's apartment and a few houses down from Françoise's place. The two women could hear the music when they were at the front of their apartment, and even more distinctly in summer than in winter.

While sitting out on her balcony last evening, Françoise saw Marie Lajoie quite by chance, walking toward the pianist on the sidewalk. The old lady stopped for a moment, smiled at the young woman and went on her way. The musician smiled back and kept on walking. A few seconds later, the two women turned and faced one another, both at the same time. They were still smiling.

A beautiful encounter was about to take place on Hutchison Street. Françoise sat down to work and didn't leave her computer once, except to go sweat intensely for a half-hour on the cardio machines at the Y. Exercising helped her to forget about her writing for a few minutes, although by the time she left the Y she was back in the clutches of her character, of course.

This morning, she woke up with Marie Lajoie and the musician lady in her head. She didn't take the time to write her dream down on paper, as she usually did, because she was in so much of a hurry to get down to work.

Her enthusiasm did not dwindle for the rest of the day.

MARIE LAJOIE

Marie Lajoie was eighty-nine years old. She thought that she still had a few good years left. The life of human beings is not eternal, she knew that, but she would have liked to be an exception. She wanted to live the longest and best life possible, and then choose the day and hour when she would die. That had been her wish since she was fifty-six.

Before the age of fifty-six, she had not been fully conscious of this thing called life, and, what's more, she had had a deep-seated fear of death. Her fear of death had had a direct impact on her life. Her subconscious played tricks on her so that her fear of death – which is so final and definitive – became entangled with all the other fears that arise in life: the fear of taking risks, asserting oneself, taking chances, losing, changing, taking action, suffering. In a word, the fear of living replaced her fear of dying and was all-consuming.

When she was fifty-six, she came to terms with death and was no longer afraid of it. She was not afraid of life or death. She understood that there was a fine line separating life from death. And that one could become the other at

233

any moment. It came to her in a dream. Another kind of person would have tried to forget about it as quickly as possible. But for Marie Lajoie it was a revelation.

In her dream, she saw herself alive, then she saw herself dead. When she woke up, she wrote an account of her dream in her journal and drew two bodies lying side by side, with a small space between them. The one on the left was alive and the one on the right was dead. But what she saw, in reality, was movement, the live body moving toward the right, and then it was over. It was dead. The live body changed its status in a fraction of a second. No pain, no fear, just a shifting over. In less than a second, memories accumulated over years of life were erased. There was no longer any memory in the dead body. The soul, the spirit, the memory, which had filled the body and kept it alive, were extinguished forever.

From that day on, she was never afraid of death anymore. But she wanted to choose the time to die. The moment at which the shift would take place, without any pain whatsoever.

From that day on, she loved life with all her strength. Since that day the only goddess she worshipped was Life, life in all its forms. And the most striking characteristic of life was that nothing remains the same as it was, that everything changes and dies.

> Only the living die.
> Only the living wither.
> Only the living change.

That day, she understood that she preferred being alive because the living are constantly changing, because the living are breathtaking, because the living are delicate and beautiful and in constant flux. Death stops everything. When something is dead it doesn't change anymore. A dead body becomes dust and, according to the scriptures, the soul awaits the last judgement or goes to heaven, purgatory, or hell, or is reincarnated, depending on what you believe in. She doesn't have any beliefs, even though she respects those who do. When you look into the abyss, you hold on to whatever you think can help.

To live in our living body with all the associated happiness and unhappiness is all that we are able to experience. Only one single time.

As Marie saw it, a dead body can no longer go up or down the stairs, it can no longer wink or smile. A dead body can no longer dance, learn a new language or be captivated by the music of Mozart, Ferré or Parker. If you are dead, you can no longer see the rays of the sun spread across your table or feel them tickle your face. A dead body can't play piano. But Marie could still do all that and feel the joy of every minute. She felt her joy grow deeper day by day, as time ran out and she had less and less time left to spend in the world of the living.

It was as if she had to settle the thorny issue of death before she could live life to the fullest. In order to move on to the most important phase in life – her last – she needed to conquer the fear that had been ruining her life.

Marie Lajoie didn't have any family left. She had survived her husband, as well as her brothers and her sisters who had all died at around a hundred or nearly – she was the youngest of them. Her only child had died at the age of four from an illness that was unknown at the time and she hadn't had other kids.

After her husband died, along with her friends, who passed away one after the other, she was lonely for a time. The only person she saw was a young neighbour she had hired to do the chores she was unable to do by herself. He lived three doors away and had become a dear friend. Julien Francoeur would be part of her life until she died, he would hold her hand the very second her heart stopped beating, when her memory would vanish forever.

Death would come when she called it – she had everything she needed on her night table – when she no longer felt like living anymore.

She had started to attend writing workshops, and she took classes in Spanish, a language that she loved and spoke fluently now. In this way, her social life had picked up again, little by little. She now had friends, and even a lover who courted her resolutely. All of them were younger than she was.

She lived alone and was rather proud of it. Like the people of the Bible, chosen by God, she felt that she, too, had been "chosen" to live Life in order to show the world that it was possible to be joyful at any age. And to think that she had had the auspicious name "Lajoie" for only sixty-five years!

Marie Latour – that was her maiden name – had been living on Hutchison Street since 1943, the year she married Charles-Henri Lajoie, an engineer. They were both working in a large architecture firm in downtown Montreal. In those days, correspondence was done almost only in English and Marie Latour was a bilingual secretary. She was so fluent in English that the first time Charles-Henri spoke to her he did so in English. "Why are you speaking English to me?" she asked, flashing her prettiest smile at him. "My name is Marie Latour and I am a French-Canadian like you." When Marie recalled the delightful moment when Charles-Henri answered her, switching to French right away, blushing and apologizing, she smiled as if he were still standing there right in front of her.

"Who will keep the image of Charles-Henri alive when I'm no longer here? Who will think about him?"

When she thought about him, about his love and his love of life, a melancholic tenderness swept through her body. When she was younger, she was besieged with melancholy, it happened often and lasted for a very long time. It was very difficult to pull herself out from under this cloud, which she dreaded and liked at the same time. But as she aged, everything happened more quickly, both the very good and the bad.

"Who will think about him? Who will think about me?"

As she evoked these tender feelings, she would try to make them last just a little longer by sitting down at the piano. For some time now, she had played without sheet music, letting her fingers, her memory, her creativity go wherever they wanted to. She would improvise until nothing else tickled her fancy. Then, she would pick up her journal and try to write down what she had never before put down in writing. It's hard work to be original, and she had the impression that it was easier to be innovative on the piano.

She had kept a diary since the age of fifteen. She had cardboard boxes filled with her notebooks, and these boxes piled up at the rate of two or three a year. Over seventy-four years, that added up to a lot of notebooks and a lot of words. A few years ago, it occurred to her that she should read her diaries again from the beginning. She spent weeks reading, reliving her life in fast forward. She had been a bit disappointed. Except for the parts where love and later death made each word resonate. From year to year, from notebook to notebook, there were few new ideas, or new emotions. She had rehashed a lot of things that had once seemed so important, but they were not, or rather they were no longer, important.

She was moved by young Marie as she discovered love. She was touched by a young woman in her first years of marriage grappling with the small and large problems of conjugal life, which took up so much space. She was overwhelmed by the death of her child, which was as heartbreaking as if it had just occurred, and also by the immeasurable sorrow of a woman losing her husband at the age of seventy-five.

The most striking change of tone came when she had

stopped fearing death, after her dream, at the age of fifty-six. It was as if a new life was beginning. A new person appeared, who looked like Marie, the child who was curious about everything, and who persevered even when she was afraid.

On her eightieth birthday, there was another surprise, at the beginning of a new notebook: "What is the use of being the actor and the only spectator in one's own life? What can I leave behind after all the years I have spent on this earth? All of my experience will die with me. My happiness and my joy will die with me. What do I have to do to leave something behind? There's a lot of pride in my desire, so many people have died without ... " She had never expressed a desire of this magnitude in any of the previous notebooks.

Then, she forgot about it, and once again began to live her life from day to day. And time passed, as if that was the only thing it could do.

Every day after breakfast, she would meditate for twenty minutes, play the piano for as long as she felt like playing, and then do a half an hour of exercise, or PE as they used to say when she was young. Then she would stand in front of the door that led to her balcony, which faced Hutchison Street. If it wasn't cold out, she would go out for a stroll or she would go out on her balcony with her cup of coffee or herbal tea. It was a beautiful day this time. From her balcony she could see a piano tied up in cables being hoisted up on the other side of the street.

A beautiful tall woman, who was excited and also some-what amused, was watching them handle the piano, which was meant to land on a third-floor balcony. As soon as the piano was put down and rolled inside the house, the young woman zoomed up the stairs. You could hear a few notes, after which the young woman went out onto the balcony with her hand over her heart. With exaggerated gestures to express her thanks, she waved to the men who were still standing on the sidewalk below. She looked happy. Marie Lajoie already liked the new arrival in the neighbourhood.

Marie heard her play on the days that followed. It wasn't classical music, or well-known tunes either, so these were surely compositions by the young woman her-self. Sometimes she accompanied herself while singing in a low voice, somewhat husky, full of warmth and ten-derness. The old woman stayed glued to her spot on the balcony and listened.

Marie Lajoie began to daydream while listening to her, and felt even more acutely her desire to leave something of herself to humanity. She had just discovered what she wanted to do: write songs.

She imagined her own words sung in the voice of this young woman. The end of a life sung with the voice of youth, a beautiful contrast and a superb way to tie togeth-er the two extremes of life.

She set about working. But how would she get start-ed? The lyrics? The music? She scratched out a few words, picked out a melody on the piano, then came back to the words. But it wasn't working. She had studied piano for about a dozen years, but had never studied composition. She had filled thousands of pages of her notebooks, but had never written poems, even though she loved to read poetry. And she had never written songs, even though she had listened to songs forever and knew dozens of them by heart. It was very challenging to become an author and composer at her age. But she wanted to take up the challenge. She wanted to leave at least one song that would withstand the test of time. At least one.

She quickly realized that writing a song had nothing to do with writing in a diary. The young woman across the street would know how to fix that, she would correct her errors. She set her journal aside and took out some blank paper just like they did in her writing workshop. She wrote for one or two hours a day. She filled the pages with scribbling, tinkering with things she wrote, but she wasn't really satisfied with anything. Not until an expression came to her: *In my forgetful mind*. She stopped and repeated the phrase. *In my forgetful mind* ... She liked that phrase. She began to hum it. She wiggled her fingers over the piano, repeating the words and letting her hands move across the keyboard ... *In my forgetful mind* ... Until the following phrase appeared ... *Dreams of childhood rewind* ...

She went to get the old typewriter that had sat idle for several years and she began to type, without making any mistakes and in one go, as if someone were dictating the words to her.

In my forgetful mind
Dreams of childhood rewind
Every instant is a commencement

In my contented mind
Each day is intertwined
With love and death drawing near
On the brink of my ninetieth year
What can I leave behind?
My love for all mankind
My friendship a legacy
For a world of agony

Time passes steadily
With only one life to live, we
Are grains of sand on the edge of the sea
Where suffering torments us endlessly

Happiness thankfully
Gives us a way to defy
The fateful end awaiting us

Remember, remember
Even pain passes eventually
We choose to bring happiness closer

Remember, remember
Time flies, but it flies too fast
Happiness is ours, we must make it last

It's the only way to shrug off
The fateful end awaiting us

Remember, remember
Time passes steadily
Even pain passes eventually
Happiness is a challenge a choice and an anchor
It's the only way to defy
The fateful death awaiting us

When she finished writing, she read it over and cried with joy, with pain. She didn't know why she was crying. She had just written her first complete song. She didn't know whether it was good or bad, but it didn't matter. What she had just written was important to her. The proof was the shiver that was running down her spine.

One year has gone by since she wrote her first song. She is soon going to celebrate her ninetieth birthday and she has just spent an extraordinary year writing songs with passion, sometimes with joy, pain, discouragement, euphoria. She has experienced all those emotions. She has finished twelve songs with a thirteenth on the way. She has decided to compose the melodies only when they come easily to her, and to concentrate on writing lyrics.

It is a beautiful day in May. Hutchison Street is sunny, the children are happy to finally be able to play in light clothing without clunky boots slowing them down. Marie Lajoie has chosen her day well. "At my age," she says to herself, "I have earned the right to refuse to be passive, to live the way I want and to die when I want. I also have the right to ask the young musician if she would like to sing my songs, knowing full well that she could easily tell me to take a hike."

Marie Lajoie walks up the stairs slowly, her shoulder bag stuffed with her papers, her cane hooked over her left arm and her right hand clinging to the railing. She stops at the door to the third floor apartment, listens with delight to the singer's voice and, as soon as it is quiet inside, rings the bell. The door opens. The young woman is surprised at first. Whenever she has run into the old lady, she has been moved by her indescribable gaze, she has been so struck by how gracious she looks that she has even turned around to watch her walk by. Like a goddess from another time. Marie Lajoie introduces herself and says that she would like to talk to her. Both shocked and touched by the presence of the old woman, the musician gives her a welcoming smile. She invites her in and gives her her arm so that she can lean on it.

FRANÇOISE CAMIRAND

Ever since she started writing about some of the people on her street, who went on to become her characters, she has started to think about the brief time in her youth when she was a model.

When she was twenty-four, she decided to travel. Paris was going to be her first big stop. She had read so many novels set in Paris that she was dying to see Saint-Germain-des-Prés, the Boul' Mich, Montparnasse, place de Fürstenberg, and all the other streets and neighbourhoods she knew the names of. So Françoise ended up in Paris, after slaving away in a trendy restaurant for an entire year. The only advantage of working as a waitress in a chichi restaurant was that even the most aggravating customers left big tips. She worked double time, saved all her money, didn't go out after work, stopped drinking and gave up the lines of coke that cost a fortune. She was a crashing bore as far as her friends were concerned, but she didn't give a damn. She had only one goal, which was to get away.

After going to the dorms for international students and dropping off her bags at the Deutsch de la Meurthe building, which took in "transients" for the summer, she went straight to Montparnasse. Excited, nervous and already awestruck, she went to La Coupole, the mythic brasserie of the books she had read, where tables were reserved for the most prominent writers and painters from Paris and elsewhere. That evening, she did not seen Jean-Paul Sartre or Simone de Beauvoir, but she did meet a painter called Stefano Cataldi, accompanied by his wife Clara, who was breathtakingly beautiful. The painter looked at her several times, then came over and asked her if she'd like to join them. She hesitated for just a moment, but then got up to sit with them. After all, she had come to Paris and to La Coupole, in particular, to meet artists, and if those two were not actually artists, they at least looked nice.

She would later call it "the first evening of my new life." It was a magnificent evening full of laughter and discovery. Right from the start, as soon as her shyness melted away, she had the feeling that she had known them forever, and she had the (well-founded) premonition that this would turn out to be a significant encounter.

A few days later, she launched into a new and fascinating experience for her — being a model. She posed for four mornings a week over a period of six months. It wasn't easy, but she learned a lot. About art, and about life.

Because while the painter is looking at his model, the model is also looking at the painter.

She witnessed the artist's concentration. He worked for four hours without flagging, at a steady rhythm, even picking up the pace sometimes. The artist's breathing was in sync with his movements. His eyes were completely transformed. He would observe her intensely, penetrating her inner self. As if he were soaking her up with his gaze and swallowing her up as he breathed.

When he stopped painting, around one o'clock in the afternoon, he was exhausted. As drained as a worker who had just finished his shift on a construction site. "I sometimes go to work in construction," he told her one day with a laugh. "It gives me a break from painting, and it works."

She was also tired, but completely spellbound. Being immobile was taxing, but she felt both weary and mesmerized as she observed the intensity with which the artist sucked up the energy he needed from his subject. Even though she was motionless, she had the feeling she was working as hard as he was.

After their working sessions, Cataldi would often invite his model to La Coupole, naturally, where he had his own table. Françoise would regain her strength and the painter would once again have a mischievous smile on his face and lapse back into his seductive chatter with a hint of an Italian accent. How many fascinating conversations they had about art and life, which were linked to one another like yin and yang, the sun and the moon, light and darkness.

Young Françoise soaked it all up.

Clara, the beautiful and generous Clara, took Françoise under her wing, showed her around Paris, introduced her to the cuisines of many countries and, best of all, encouraged her to talk. Françoise was the kind of person that people referred to as a party girl – she liked to laugh, have a good time and drink. But, deep down, she didn't open up easily, her anxiety made her clam up as indescribable emotions bubbled up inside her. Clara's intelligent and gentle nature turned out to be beneficial because she helped Françoise to understand why she was floundering and to become more conscious of her fears and desires. While Françoise was walking around Île Saint-Louis with Clara, after she had been living in Paris for around six months, it dawned on her that one day she would have to deal with her fears if she wanted to fulfil her dreams. It was inevitable. She couldn't get around it without giving it a try. She had to try, at least. Her entire body quivered with terror, and she knew at that very moment that if she ever managed to control her anxieties, she would get her life back. Her real life. The one she wanted to live.

Through Cataldi and Clara she met many painters, writers and musicians. There were elaborate dinners cooked by Clara, who was a talented chef. That year, she had handed over responsibility for a restaurant she was running to her assistant, which gave her the time she needed to come up with new recipes. During one of her famous and unforgettable meals, Françoise heard a painter say to a writer, "When an artist paints a portrait, he is always painting himself." While the writer was mulling this over, Cataldi jumped into the conversation and agreed. Absolutely no doubt, he opined. Françoise didn't understand. She could see herself in Cataldi's portraits, and even when he had painted only one part of her body, it was her, good God, and no one else.

She was young then, and had not yet started to write.

It was not until she wrote this book – until it was practically all finished – that she fully grasped what she had heard at the age of twenty-four. If Cataldi had chosen her, it was probably because he saw in her a part of himself that he had not yet explored. You are only conscious of something that is already part of your subconscious, perhaps unknowingly. Consciousness – from *con* ("together") and *scire* ("to know") – is a joint process.

And that's what Françoise had being doing right from the beginning.

All of the characters she portrayed were part of herself. Threads of the lives of others or threads of her own life – it didn't matter – which she wove together to form the fabric of life itself.

As her printer spews out the pages of her book, she is as excited as she was the very first time. She feels the urge to pick up the phone and call Jean-Hugues, to say, "come over and bring a bottle of champagne, my novel is finished!" Except that her lover is sulking at the moment. It's not hard to figure out why. She didn't want to talk about what she was writing and, mainly, she didn't let him read the manuscript before anyone else. Not even one paragraph. This is the first time this has happened since they got together.

The main reason is that this novel is very different from her previous ones. That's what she wanted. Even though she trusts him utterly, she was afraid he would interfere, that he would exert his influence one way or the other. She is more vulnerable than she looks. Secondly, Jean-Hugues is *in* the novel. She hasn't told him yet. She has changed his name, of course, but everyone will recognize her publisher, who is a public figure.

She doesn't want any reactions. If she had allowed him to read the book, she would have had to do the same for the twenty other people who inspired her. It was out of the question, and even impossible, in certain cases. She wanted to be fair to everyone, even though she was motivated by trepidation more than anything else. "*C'est ça qui est ça,*" as Martin Léon says in his song. That's just the way it is. When the pages are bound together, into an actual paperback book, she will feel strong, that's what she's hoping. No one will be able to change anything after that. And if Jean-Hugues refuses to publish it, she will go elsewhere.

As she hugs her stack of pages and the characters they evoke, she is singing out loud, belting out lines of a Vigneault song about ships making love and waging war amid the crashing waves.[8] She pours herself a glass of wine, fills a dish with salted almonds, and goes out onto her balcony. It is the middle of May. Except for a two-week break to tour universities in Mexico, a week in New York at the invitation of the PEN and a few appearances at Montreal libraries, she has spent the past year, to the day, writing about her street, spurred on by Hinda Rochel, who came to her in her dreams night after night.

Madeleine Desrochers is walking along, holding onto Nzimbou's arm, Benoît Fortin sprints past them, Chawki and Isabelle are going home, teasing one another and laughing, a few young Hasidim race past as if they were going to put out a fire somewhere, and Hinda Rochel is coming home from school.

Just before stepping into her house, Hinda Rochel turns around and spots Françoise, who waves to her and smiles.

After brushing the *mezuzah* with her hand, and before slipping inside, Hinda Rochel looks up at Françoise once more, with a smile on her face.

It is a timid smile, but it is beautiful.

ENDNOTES

[1] Gabrielle Roy (1909–1983) was one of French Canada's most prominent authors. Her first novel, *Bonheur d'occasion*, was published in 1945 and was translated into English as *The Tin Flute*, first by Hannah Josephson in 1947, then by Alan Brown in 1980.

[2] *Pendant que,* written by legendary Quebec singer/songwriter Gilles Vigneault.

[3] In this song, the French singer Renaud reminisces about his past, one of the features of which is a candy called "*mistral gagnant*"; some of the packages were marked "*gagnant*," meaning that another package could be obtained free.

[4] *Toujours vivant* was composed by Michel Rivard, with lyrics by Gerry Boulet.

[5] Fool around; mess up; bother; flip flops; wuss; hooker.

[6] Snow banks; slush; black ice; blowing snow.

[7] Gabrielle Roy's autobiographical novel *Ces enfants*

de ma vie(1977) was translated by Alan Brown as *Children of My Heart* (McClelland and Stewart, 1979). This quote is taken from Brown's translation. The original French reads as follows: "*En repassant, comme il m'arrive souvent, ces temps-ci, par mes années de jeune institutrice, dans une école de garçons, en ville, je revis, toujours aussi chargé d'émotion, le matin de la rentrée. J'avais la classe des tout-petits.*"

8 This is another reference to *Pendant que*, by Gilles Vigneault.